Broken Promises

D1008399

Cedar River Daydreams (for girls 12–15):

#1 *New Girl in Town*
#2 *Trouble with a Capital "T"*
#3 *Jennifer's Secret*
#4 *Journey to Nowhere*
#5 *Broken Promises*
#6 *The Intruder*
#7 *Silent Tears No More*
#8 *Fill My Empty Heart*

Springflower Books (for girls 12–15):

Adrienne   *Melissa*
Erica   *Michelle*
Jill   *Paige*
Laina   *Sara*
Lisa   *Wendy*
Marty

Heartsong Books (for young adults):

Andrea   *Kara*
Anne   *Karen*
Carrie   *Leslie*
Colleen   *Rachel*
Cynthia   *Shelly*
Gillian   *Sherri*
Jenny   *Stacey*
Jocelyn   *Tiffany*

Broken Promises

Judy Baer

BETHANY HOUSE PUBLISHERS
MINNEAPOLIS, MINNESOTA 55438
A Division of Bethany Fellowship, Inc.

Broken Promises
Judy Baer

Library of Congress Catalog Card Number 89-61629

ISBN 1-55661-087-4

Published by Bethany House Publishers
A Division of Bethany Fellowship, Inc.
6820 Auto Club Road, Minneapolis, Minnesota 55438

Printed in the United States of America

For Pam Muelhbauer and P. J. Baerbauer
Two of my favorite people!

JUDY BAER received a B.A. in English and Education from Concordia College in Moorhead, Minnesota. She has had fifteen novels published and is a member of the National Romance Writers of America, the Society of Children's Book Writers and the National Federation of Press Women.

Two of her novels have been prizewinning best-sellers in the Bethany House SPRINGFLOWER SERIES (for girls 12–15); *Adrienne* and *Paige*. Both books have been awarded first place for juvenile fiction in the National Federation of Press Women's communications contest.

Chapter One

"Those two are always together. If I didn't know better I'd think they were born Siamese twins," Jennifer Golden commented sourly as she watched Peggy Madison and Chad Allen walk together down the hallway of Cedar River High School. "They're like bookends. You never see one without the other."

Lexi Leighton remained silent as she watched Peggy's and Chad's receding backs. The couple was holding hands and gazing into each other's eyes, oblivious to the controlled chaos of the school hallway between classes.

"It does seem like forever since Peggy and I have spent any time together," Lexi finally acknowledged. "Either I'm too busy or—"

"It's not you that's too busy," Jennifer huffed and scraped her blond bangs away from her eyes. "She's so wrapped up in Chad that when I call her on the telephone she asks me to hang up so she can wait for his call."

Lexi nodded as she pulled her history book out of the locker. A troubled expression darkened her brown eyes and marred her pretty features. "I'm surprised they even have time to talk on the phone. Except for Peggy's basketball practice, they're always together."

"That just tells you how important the team is to Peggy," Jennifer pointed out. "She'd be flying high if she were sure she could start for Cedar River."

"I guess we should be glad she has other interests," Lexi commented mildly. "Other than Chad."

Jennifer pushed her locker door shut with a resounding slam. "Maybe I'm just jealous, but I think it's sick. Sometimes I'm embarrassed to be around them. I liked Peggy better before she got so serious about Chad." Then Jennifer turned an appraising eye to Lexi. "I'm glad you and Todd Winston aren't sickening like they are."

"You know how strict my parents are, Jen. I'd be grounded for life if I pulled something like that." Lexi's smile softened the words.

"For life? That *is* strict!"

They were laughing as they made their way to the next classroom, but Lexi's mind kept returning to Jennifer's angry words.

It embarrasses me to be around them. . . . I liked Peggy better before she got so serious about Chad. . . . Much as Lexi hated to admit it, she was beginning to feel the same way Jennifer did. Peggy wasn't nearly as much fun as she used to be. Chad was a nice boy, but he'd certainly taken over all of Peggy's free time.

Lexi had difficulty following Mr. Raddis as he droned on about the Civil War. Instead, her mind wandered to her conversation with Jennifer. Lexi found herself doodling her name and Todd's on the inside cover of her notebook. Fortunately, her relationship with Todd was much different from Chad and Peggy's. Most importantly, she and Todd were friends. They enjoyed being together, but their relationship hadn't developed the intensity that Peggy and Chad's had. Jennifer was right. Peggy and Chad's relationship made Lexi uncomfortable too.

Lexi reached into her pocket for a tissue and her fingers curled around a canister of film she'd taken of the girls' basketball team for the *River Review*. She glanced at the clock on the wall. If she took the film down to the newsroom in her free period after history, there would still be time to get it developed today. When the bell rang after class, Lexi gathered her books and darted out of the room.

The newsroom was dark, with the shades pulled to keep out the sun.

That was odd, Lexi mused. When the paper staff was at work, there were always windows open and radios blaring. Mrs. Drummond rarely pulled the shades. Lexi moved into the room whistling softly to herself and was startled at the sound of frenzied scurrying in the far corner of the room.

As her eyes adjusted to the dimness, Lexi could see Chad and Peggy unwinding themselves from a romantic clinch. Their faces were flushed to an embarrassed pink. Chad scrubbed roughly at his lips to remove the traces of Peggy's pale peach lipstick.

"I—I—didn't realize anyone was in here," Lexi stammered, blushing herself.

Peggy adjusted her sweater as she moved toward Lexi. "I guess we shouldn't have been in here, but it was empty and . . ." She gave a helpless shrug as if to indicate that they were forced into the room and into each other's arms.

"The photography students will be by any minute to pick up the film to develop," Lexi reminded them softly.

"We'd better go," Chad murmured. He looked less embarrassed than Peggy at being caught, but even he brushed by Lexi with his head down, refusing to meet her eyes.

"Chad! Wait up!" Peggy grabbed her books off the table by the door. "Thanks for the warning, Lexi." And she was gone.

Slowly, Lexi moved toward Mrs. Drummond's desk and dropped the film canister into the basket marked "To Develop." Before she'd even had a chance to leave the room, Tim Anders, a photography student who developed many of her photos, dashed into the room and scooped up the film.

Lexi was in a thoughtful mood as she returned to study hall. If she hadn't caught Peggy and Chad in that stupid, compromising situation, Tim would have. And Tim was far more likely to tease Chad and let the world know what he'd found than Lexi was. Peggy was becoming very indiscreet. The idea bothered Lexi a great deal.

Peggy found Lexi in the hallway after school, cleaning her locker. Most of the students had already left the building.

"Thanks."

Lexi looked up from the stack of books and papers spread on the floor. "For what?"

"For not making a big deal about finding Chad and me . . . you know."

Lexi organized the books and lifted them back into her locker. "I felt really stupid walking in on you like that."

Peggy shrugged. "Yeah, well, we probably should have gone to the furnace room like we usually do but—" She stopped, realizing she'd given away a secret.

"You do that in the furnace room too?" Lexi echoed. "What if you get caught?"

"By Mr. Hauser? The janitor? He wouldn't care. Anyway, we just like to spend time together, that's all."

"Well, I think it's ridiculous."

Peggy appeared startled at Lexi's frank statement. Her expression turned to a frown. "What's *that* supposed to mean?"

"I just think it's inappropriate, that's all. This is a high school, not the backseat of a car!"

With a hostility that Lexi had never before heard in her friend's voice, Peggy retorted, "Well, Little Miss High and Mighty, you can decide what's 'appropriate' for you but don't try and decide for me!"

"What happened to us, Peggy?" Lexi pleaded. "We used to be friends who could tell each other everything. Now you're so distant and so . . . angry."

"I'm angry because you made me that way," Peggy said shortly. "I expected better from you, Lexi Leighton. You have no business telling me what I can or can't do! I'll be with Chad whenever and wherever I choose. And I'll do what I want—no matter what you say!" Peggy's face had turned a ruddy pink and her eyes were flashing.

"I'm not trying to run your life, if that's what you

think, Peggy. I just think there are other times and place—"

"Hah! Not for you, Goody-Two Shoes. I know how you are." A bell rang in the hallway and Peggy looked down at her wristwatch. "Terrific. Now I'm going to be late for basketball practice. Now the Coach will be mad." Without another word she turned and ran away.

With a heavy heart, Lexi walked to the newsroom. Now it was bustling with activity. Egg Mc-Naughton was tinkering with page layout as Minda Hannaford held court in one corner, giving her ideas for her next column. Several others were at their jobs as well. Lexi sat down at a typewriter and began to type captions for the photos in the next edition of the *River Review*.

It was almost five o'clock when she finished. There were only a few minutes left of basketball practice when Lexi meandered into the gymnasium and crawled to the top sections of the bleachers to watch.

Cedar River had an excellent girls' basketball team. Peggy was one of the tallest. Her long legs were well-shaped and she looked very athletic in her uniform. She was graceful and well-coordinated—a force to be reckoned with on the basketball court.

"You alone?" Jennifer flung herself down on the bleacher next to Lexi. "What are you looking at?"

"I was just thinking about Peggy. She looks great, doesn't she?"

Jennifer bobbed her head in agreement. "Rumor has it that she'll be in the starting lineup this fall if she keeps on playing like she has been."

"I guess so. I heard that there's still a question about Peggy because she's only a sophomore, but I know how much she wants that position." *And maybe being a starter will get her mind off Chad, even for a little while.* Though both girls were thinking the same thing, they left the words unsaid.

"Are you staying?" Jennifer wondered.

"Yeah. I just finished up in the newsroom and thought I'd watch the rest of practice."

"I just took a test." Jennifer wrinkled her nose. "What a hassle."

Because she was dyslexic, Jennifer often took oral tests.

"You think you've got hassles," Lexi muttered.

"Troubles?"

"Peggy."

"Peggy and *Chad*, you mean."

"Same thing."

"Don't I know it."

"I wish we could be close friends again."

"There's no room," Jennifer observed frankly. "Chad's taking up all the space around her."

"I didn't realize that could happen with friends," Lexi murmured, "but I guess it can."

Rather than comment, Jennifer changed the subject. "Matt Windsor called last night."

"Really? How's he doing? I don't see him much around school." Matt and Jennifer had gone through a very rebellious stage together.

"He's okay. Says he's trying really hard to get along with his stepmother. I guess they even went to church together last week."

"That's a switch. Good for him."

Jennifer nodded and the two girls stared awhile longer at the basketball court. Finally Jennifer observed, "I noticed Egg and Minda were in the cafeteria at the same time today and he didn't offer to carry her tray or mop up her spilt milk with his shirt or anything."

Lexi didn't try to hide her grin at Jennifer's graphic description of the way Egg and Minda interacted. Egg had a wild and hopeless crush on Minda even though Minda didn't seem to know poor Egg existed.

"Todd and I keep telling Egg that the way to get Minda interested in him is to act as if he's *not* interested in her."

"Do you believe that?"

"I'm not sure, but I can't stand to see Egg make a fool of himself anymore. Whatever works."

"Poor Egg." Jennifer shook her head. "He could have picked just about anyone else in the school and they would have liked him just 'cause he's so sweet . . . but Minda!"

"Sometimes I think Minda doesn't like anyone—including herself," Lexi observed. Minda Hannaford was one of the unhappiest—and often most malicious—people she'd ever met.

"Just so Egg can keep his head on about her," Jennifer observed practically. "Otherwise he's setting himself up for heartbreak."

Lexi sighed and stared straight ahead. Life was more complicated than she'd ever dreamed it could be.

Practice ended and the players headed for the showers. Slowly Lexi and Jennifer made their way out of the gym and to the lockers. They'd gathered their jackets and books when a voice sang out behind them.

"Hey! Wait up!"

It was Peggy, her hair still wet, her clothes hurriedly pulled on. "Are you walking my way?"

"Sure." Lexi smiled, relieved to see that Peggy had cooled down after their confrontation.

Peggy shook her head and droplets of water flew everywhere.

"Hey! My dog does that when he gets wet!" Jennifer protested. "Lay off."

Peggy grinned and shook her head again. "How about stopping at the Hamburger Shack?" she asked. "I'd love a malt."

"Before supper?"

"Of course. I've run about fifty miles in practice."

"For a few minutes," Jennifer agreed. "How about you, Lexi?"

"Sure. Mom said she'd have supper late because I didn't know how long I'd be at school."

At the Hamburger Shack, the three girls wound their way through the tables to a booth at the back. Peggy ordered a malt and a large fries, while Lexi and Jennifer settled on small soft drinks.

"I hear you might play on the varsity team!" Jennifer announced.

Peggy crossed her fingers in front of her nose. "Keep hoping. I want to be one of the starting five so badly I can just *taste* it!"

This is just like it used to be, Lexi thought to herself as Peggy and Jennifer debated the chances of the girls' team going to state this year. *Just like it used to be . . . before Chad.*

As if Jennifer had read Lexi's mind, she blurted, "Where's Chad tonight? Doesn't he usually pick you up after practice?"

"Oh, he had to run some errands for his dad. He didn't think he'd be done in time to pick me up. I'll talk to him later."

Lexi had no doubt of that.

"Have you heard my latest news?" Peggy asked, her eyes shining.

"You got a car!" Jennifer teased.

"This is better."

"Better than a car? Wow! What is it?"

"I might be going to London!"

Both Lexi and Jennifer did a double take at that comment.

"When?"

"How?"

"Why?"

Peggy laughed and held up her hands. "Slow down and I'll tell you." She swabbed a french fry through the catsup on her plate.

"You know that my dad teaches at the junior college, right?"

Lexi and Peggy nodded.

"Well, he's had an opportunity to go to London and do some research for a book he's been writing. He's not sure when he'll be able to leave, but he thinks it will be enough of a learning experience that he's willing to take me out of school so I can go along. Isn't that great?"

"I guess so! London!"

"Yeah. Of course, it all depends on how long he has to stay to get his research done." Then Peggy's expression turned dreamy. "The first place I'd go is Buckingham Palace."

"I'd go to the Tower of London. I loved studying about that in history class."

"Do you think Charles and Di will be in town? Maybe you could drop in for tea."

"Or go shopping with her for Wills!"

"And borrow some of her used dresses!"

Soon the three were giggling so hard they couldn't talk.

Then Peggy shoved her plate away and stood up. "Dad will never take me to London if I don't get home for supper, though. It was good to talk."

They walked three blocks together before Jennifer turned off onto her own street.

"Lexi," she called over her shoulder, "don't forget we're going to try out for the Emerald Tones at eight-thirty. In the music room. See you there!"

With a nod and a wave, Lexi and Peggy continued on their way in silent, comfortable camaraderie. When she said goodbye to Peggy, Lexi felt happier and more lighthearted about their friendship than she had for many weeks.

Chapter Two

Every light in the Leighton household was on Lexi noted as she approached the front door. Her little brother Ben greeted her with a cheerful "Hi, Lexi."

"Hi, yourself. How was school today?"

"Fun," Ben answered happily.

Lexi smiled. Every day was fun for Ben in his first year at the Academy for the Handicapped. He had made dozens of new friends, several of whom had Down's syndrome just like he did. Sometimes, Lexi mused, Ben had a more active social life than she.

Eagerly he took her by the hand and led her down the hallway toward the kitchen where her mother and father were putting the finishing touches on the dinner table.

"There you are," Mrs. Leighton said. "Just in time. I'll mash the potatoes while you pour water in the glasses and we'll all sit up to eat."

Lexi sank gratefully into her chair. The kitchen was full of wonderful smells. Roast beef and carrots from the oven, freshly baked rolls and a pie cooling on the counter. Her mother had gone all out for dinner tonight. Mrs. Leighton had been doing that a lot lately. This morning, she'd been baking muffins and cooking oatmeal before Lexi's alarm went off.

Her parents took their places at the table and Mr. Leighton looked from his wife to Lexi and then to Ben. "Ben, would you like to say grace for us this evening?" Ben's dark eyes sparkled and he nodded his head so enthusiastically that his chair shook a little.

"Ben will do it. Ben will pray," he said with great satisfaction. Solemnly he folded his hands and bowed his head until Lexi could see only the shiny dark crown of his head.

"Thanks, God," Ben began, "for meat and for potatoes and for carrots and"—his eyes darted up and he looked around to see what else was on the table—"and pie." He paused for a long moment before adding, ". . . and Lexi and Mom and Dad and Ben. Amen."

Lexi bent low over her plate to hide her smile. She loved to listen to Ben's prayers. They were so sincere and so forthright and so immediate. She was very proud of Ben for mastering language skills. He'd struggled many hours with his parents while learning the Lord's Prayer, but now he could say it with more sincerity and more emotion than anyone else she'd ever heard.

For the next few minutes, the Leightons were relatively quiet, enjoying the meal Mrs. Leighton had cooked. Then Lexi's father laid his fork across the top of the plate and looked at her thoughtfully.

"What is it, Dad?" she asked. "What are you thinking about?"

"Just thinking about you, Lexi. About how grown up and mature you've become since we've moved to Cedar River. One of these days, I'm going look up and realize that you're ready for college."

Lexi felt a little blush of pleasure rising in her cheeks. "I think you've got awhile before that happens."

"Somewhere along the line we've got to start thinking about saving for college."

"Let's not start today!" Mrs. Leighton chimed in. "I get depressed just thinking about it!"

"I do think," Mr. Leighton continued, "that I'd feel better if we knew that you were putting some money away for college. Ben's schooling at the Academy is very expensive and with two of you in school, your mom and I might have to tighten our belts considerably if we don't start saving now."

Lexi looked at her slender mother who was wearing jeans and a pastel shirt tucked in at her waist. She hardly looked old enough to have a daughter thinking about college days.

Suddenly, Mrs. Leighton jabbed a fork into a potato with a vengeance. "I don't like it."

Lexi stared at her in bewilderment.

"I don't like the idea one bit," Mrs. Leighton complained. "I hate the thought of Lexi going to college. I'm already beginning to feel useless around here."

Ben gave his mother a worried glance. He didn't comprehend what was going on, but he knew he didn't like her tone.

"What do you mean by that, Mom?" Lexi wondered.

Mrs. Leighton's shoulders sagged. "I just feel so

unneeded now that both you and Ben are gone all day long." Her hand swept across the table. "I can't be cooking huge meals all the time. My freezer's full of baking and I've sewn new curtains for every bedroom." Mrs. Leighton crossed her hands across her chest. "Sometimes I feel so useless."

Ben's eyes were wide as saucers. "Mommy's useless?" he echoed. "What's useless?"

A crooked smile tugged at the corner of Mrs. Leighton's lip. "Oh, Ben, I don't think Mommy *is* useless, but sometimes she *feels* useless. She feels as if you don't need her to take care of you anymore."

Ben's head bobbed up and down. "Ben needs Mommy."

"And Lexi does too! Mom, that's a crazy idea," Lexi interjected. "This house wouldn't run without you. Isn't that right, Dad?"

Mr. Leighton nodded emphatically.

"Maybe," her mother said doubtfully. Then she shook her head. "Never mind me. Perhaps this is just a phase, something I'll grow out of."

"That's what you tell me all the time, Mom. That I'll grow out of it. I hope it's true for you too, because you're definitely needed around here."

Lexi's father had been quiet all through the exchange. Now, he cleared his throat and tapped the index finger of his right hand against his water glass. "May I make a suggestion?"

Three pairs of eyes turned toward him.

"I think you need more to occupy your time."

His wife rolled her eyes. "Isn't that what I just said? The kids are growing away from me—"

"I think you're going to have to start something

new. A new hobby, a new interest, join a new club."

"Yeah, Mom. You haven't done any oil painting for quite awhile. You used to do a lot of it when we lived in Grover's Point."

Mrs. Leighton nodded thoughtfully. "True. The only time I've touched my easel lately is to dust it."

"Well, why don't you dust it off one more time," her husband suggested, "and then put a canvas on it and do some painting. I should think you'd enjoy getting back to your art in a more serious way."

"Yeah, Mom. You told me once that you gave up painting because we were too small and it made such a terrible mess," Lexi pointed out. "We're not too small any longer. You *should* start painting again."

Mrs. Leighton's eyes had brightened considerably during the course of the conversation. She was nodding her head with growing enthusiasm.

"You know? You're absolutely right. I've been sitting home feeling sorry for myself when I have an opportunity for something to do right under my very nose. In fact," and she pushed away from the table and jumped up, "I got something in the mail today."

She hurried to the counter and sorted through the letters in a small wicker basket. "Here it is. There's going to be a juried art show right here in Cedar River in less than a month. There's an entry application included." She waved the sheet of paper in the air. "The deadline is tomorrow. I still have time to mail it in."

"That's a great idea, Mom," Lexi encouraged her. "What would you enter?"

Her mother shrugged. "Well, I don't know . . . yet. I'd have to paint something. I could enter my works as untitled and do that later."

"Go for it, Mom," Lexi urged.

"Gopher, gopher," Ben echoed.

Mrs. Leighton looked from Lexi to her husband. "If you two wouldn't mind. Maybe I'll just go dig out some of those oil paints right now. I wonder if all my tubes are dried up." She glanced at her watch. "If they are, I'll need to get some new ones, and there's an art and crafts shop over on Higgins that's open until nine."

"We'll do the dishes, Mom," Lexi promised. "You just go check out your paints."

Mrs. Leighton left the kitchen, muttering, "I certainly hope I have a canvas already stretched. Now that I'm in the mood, I really hate to take the time to do that . . ."

Lexi and her dad began to chuckle as soon as Mrs. Leighton had disappeared from sight. "I didn't realize she was so unhappy," Lexi said.

Her father shook his head. "Your mother just wants to be busy. She likes to be doing things for people. I'm sure it has been hard on her seeing you and Ben become so independent. Actually, this might turn out to be a good thing. I'm delighted to see her getting back to painting. She's very talented." Then he crossed his arms over his chest and leaned back in his chair looking fondly at Lexi. "In fact, my family is filled with talented women."

———

Ben helped Lexi clean the kitchen. After loading the dishwasher and wiping the counters, Lexi set out for the Emerald Tones' tryouts in the music room of the school. The closer she got to the appointed room, the louder became the sound of voices warming up.

The Emerald Tones had received statewide recognition. That fact made the butterfly wings in Lexi's stomach flap a little harder. It would be devastating not to be accepted—especially since Todd was already a member and counting on her becoming a part of the group.

Inside the music room Lexi's favorite teacher, Mrs. Waverly, was directing traffic. Mrs. Waverly was fair, unflappable and infinitely patient. Her beige hair, piled high on top of her head, bounced slightly as she separated the boys from the girls and the sopranos from the altos in an effort to make some order of the room.

Jennifer sauntered up beside Lexi with a worried look on her face. "Hi. Are you nervous?"

"Terrified," Lexi admitted. "I think it's because I want to be in this group so badly that if I don't make it . . ."

Jennifer nodded sagely. "I know exactly what you mean. I feel the same way. Being one of the Emerald Tones is a real status thing around school."

Lexi cocked one eyebrow. "You mean like being a Hi-Five?" she asked. Hi-Five was a club of very status conscious, snobbish girls who greeted one another by slapping their right hands together high over their heads.

Jennifer winced. "Yeah, maybe you're right. Status things aren't always the greatest things to be a part of."

Lexi smiled. "Oh, they're fun to be a part of, all right, but they aren't the most important things in the world." Then she clamped her hands across her stomach. "I wish my stomach would believe me when I say that."

"May I have your attention please?" Mrs. Waverly announced. "Would those of you who ordered jackets please come and try them on? For those of you waiting to try out for the Emerald Tones for the first time, would you please take seats at the back of the room."

Once again, chaos ensued as everyone lunged for their emerald green double-breasted wool jackets.

"Don't they look great?" Jennifer sighed. "I want one of those jackets in the worst possible way."

"I thought everyone had to try out for the Emerald Tones every year," Lexi puzzled. "Why is it that some are ordering and trying on jackets and the rest of us are sitting back here having nervous breakdowns?"

Jennifer chuckled. "Everyone has to try out every year, but it's pretty common knowledge that you don't get into the Emerald Tones unless you're good enough to stay in. That's why they let people order their own jackets. You can use it for as many years as you're in the group before turning it in."

"So you mean if we make it this time, we're in for the rest of our high school years?"

"More or less," Jennifer nodded. "Good deal, huh? The older members just try out for appearance's sake."

"No wonder they can afford to be so casual about this," Lexi commented, "if they already know that they're going to be accepted."

"Yeah," Jennifer agreed, "but the down side is that all of us sitting back here quaking in our boots *aren't* going to be accepted. They choose only five or six new members a year."

Lexi looked at the nervous group awaiting tryouts. "There must be forty or fifty kids here," she gasped.

"Yup, and only one in ten will be an Emerald Tone. Pretty depressing, huh?"

A wave of panic flooded over Lexi. What was she doing here, anyway? She couldn't keep up with these kids!

Lexi was deciding that it would be smarter for her to stay home and take up painting with her mother than to attempt to get into a group as elite and tightly knit as this one when Todd Winston sauntered into the room. He glanced around, his blue eyes settling first on one person then another until he connected with Lexi. His expression brightened and with a warm look he gave her a confident thumbs-up sign that made her spirits soar.

Todd thought she could do it. *He* had confidence in her. Lexi took a deep breath. If Todd thought she could make the Emerald Tones, then she knew she could.

Last year's Emerald Tone members tried out first and Lexi had the opportunity to hear the quality of the voices in the group. Then, the newcomers auditioned. She and Jennifer had to sing about halfway through the second group.

By the time it was her turn, Lexi was so nervous, her knees were wobbling like rubber hoses. She was terrified that her voice would not work at all. But when the moment came to sing out, she could hear her voice loud, clear and melodious, sounding as if it came from somewhere other than inside herself.

Todd met her out in the hallway after the tryouts. "Hey! You were great. I don't think I've ever heard you sing any better than that."

"Thanks. I was afraid I'd faint. I was so nervous."

He chuckled. "Everyone is. It's a big deal to get into the Emerald Tones."

"When are we going to find out who makes it and who doesn't?" Lexi wondered.

"Mrs. Waverly will post the new members of the Emerald Tones on the central bulletin board some time tomorrow."

Jennifer, coming up beside them, heard Todd's answer and groaned. "Tomorrow? You mean we have to wait until *tomorrow*?" She put her hand to her forehead in mock dismay. "That means I won't sleep a wink tonight. I'll be in absolute torture."

"Aren't you overreacting?" Todd asked Jennifer mildly. "Even just a little bit?"

Jennifer turned to Lexi. "Well, do you think I am, Lexi?"

Lexi was quiet a long moment as she contemplated the fact that her stomach was tying and untying itself in huge knots. "Now I know how Peggy feels waiting to hear if she's made the basketball team."

Todd flung an arm around each of the girls' shoulders. "Have some faith in yourselves!"

Easier said than done, Lexi thought ruefully. Until this moment, she hadn't realized how important it was to her that she become an Emerald Tone after all.

Chapter Three

"If you girls are so nervous, I think you'd better let me try to distract you," Todd offered cheerfully, aware of Jennifer and Lexi's jitters. "Let's go to the Hamburger Shack. I could use some greasy fries and a milk shake."

"Sure!" Jennifer chimed in quickly. "I think we both deserve a reward for getting through tryouts without coming apart at the seams."

"Just so I'm home by ten," Lexi warned. "Dad said not a minute later."

Todd glanced at his watch. "No problem. I'll have you there on time."

The Hamburger Shack was busier now than it had been earlier in the day. Jerry Randall was working behind the counter. He smiled and waved as Todd led the way to a booth. Jennifer and Lexi slipped into one side and Todd sat directly across from them.

"Jerry's pretty friendly today," Lexi observed.

"Yeah, usually he's so serious. He's been an old grump ever since that accident." Then Jennifer

29

glanced contritely at Lexi. "Whoops. I didn't mean to bring that up."

Lexi shrugged. "It's okay." She didn't like to think about the time Jerry had been racing and had hit her brother Ben with his car. "I wonder what he's so happy about today?"

"Looks like he's coming this way. Why don't you ask him?" Todd said.

Jerry arrived at their table and pulled the pencil from behind his ear and the note pad from his back pocket. "Hi. I'm waiting tables tonight besides working behind the counter. What can I get you?"

After they'd ordered, Todd ventured, "Must be a good day, Randall. I haven't seen you with that big a smile on your face in months."

"My parents are coming home."

"Really?" Jennifer's eyes grew wide. "They haven't been home for a long time, have they?"

Jerry's parents were both engineers who worked for an oil company. They had traveled most of Jerry's teenage life while he had lived in Cedar River with an uncle and aunt.

Jerry smiled with pleasure and Lexi was reminded what a handsome guy Jerry could be when he lost his sullen expression.

"It'll be great. It's been months since I've seen them. I think this time they're going to stay. My dad says he's getting sick of traveling all the time and he'd like to get back to a normal home life."

"That would be great for you, wouldn't it, Jerry?" Lexi said softly. "I'd hate to have my parents gone all the time."

"Yeah," he nodded and Lexi noticed a flicker of

pain. "It's been hard, but things are going to be better now. I know they are." He ran his fingers through his dark hair and squared his wide, athletic shoulders. "I'd better get this order in so you can eat."

After Jerry had left the table, Lexi noticed that Todd's eyes were troubled. He was folding and unfolding his straw wrapper. "Is something wrong?" she asked.

He angled his head in the direction Jerry had taken. "I was just thinking about Randall. He's setting himself up for a big disappointment."

"What do you mean?" Jennifer wondered.

"It's just that every time Jerry's parents come home, he tells someone that he thinks they're going to stay. And every time, they leave again without making any plans for coming back to the States permanently. I just hope he isn't disappointed again."

"If I had a kid, I wouldn't leave him like that," Jennifer announced bluntly.

"No, I wouldn't either," Lexi agreed. "When I first met Jerry, I didn't realize what a tough life he'd had."

Todd nodded. "Parents really cramp our style sometimes, but I'd rather be with them than without them."

The somber mood of the three was jarred by the sound of screaming and squealing in the far booth where a group of Hi-Fives had gathered. Between their flashy clothes and the noise they were making, the Hi-Fives were hard to ignore.

Todd glanced their way for a moment and then back to Lexi and Jennifer. He tilted his head toward the group of Hi-Five girls. "Do either of you have anything to do with anyone in that club anymore?"

Jennifer answered with an unladylike snort. "Are you kidding? Every member of the Hi-Fives acts like Lexi and I are invisible. If we were wiped off the face of the planet tomorrow, they wouldn't bat an eyelash."

"It's not that bad," Lexi protested unconvincingly, although deep down inside she had to admit that it did hurt.

"Well, you know how Minda Hannaford treats Lexi," Jennifer pointed out.

Todd chuckled. "Minda treats everyone that way."

"Right," Jennifer scoffed. "Your basic teenage girl with a heart of stone."

Lexi remained silent. She and Minda had been through a lot together. Minda was a complicated personality and Lexi felt that someday, perhaps under other circumstances, she and Minda might even be friends. But as long as there was a Hi-Five, that prospect seemed not only unlikely but impossible.

Lexi watched as the members of the Hi-Five club vied for the attention of a table full of boys near their booth. She wondered sometimes if she ever would have become involved with the Hi-Fives had she been less lonely and impatient for friends when she first moved to Cedar River. As it was, when they'd asked her to steal as her initiation into the club, she'd had to refuse. By doing that she'd embarrassed and shamed them and made enemies rather than friends.

Lexi had chosen not to become a Hi-Five even though they tended to be mean and thoughtless to girls who were not one of their inner circle.

Lexi and her friends had just finished up the last

of their order and were preparing to leave when Peggy Madison and her boyfriend, Chad, entered the Hamburger Shack.

Lexi blinked as she stared at the couple. They both looked very disheveled. Peggy's hair was a mess and her clothes were rumpled.

Lexi glanced away. Her stomach was knotting up again. Staring at Chad was no less disconcerting. His pale brown hair was also a mess, and he wore a self-satisfied grin on his face.

Just staring at them made Lexi feel as though she'd intruded on something highly personal.

Jennifer gave a soft snort. "The least they could have done was comb their hair and straighten their clothes before coming in here." Her voice and posture radiated disapproval.

"Shhh," Lexi whispered; "they might hear you."

"I don't care if they do," Jennifer said even more loudly. "Everybody knows that they've been making out in Chad's car all night, but they don't have to go and advertise it besides. It's a little like saying 'Look at us! See how far we've gone.' "

Lexi felt herself blushing. She'd wondered several times herself just how far Peggy and Chad *had* gone. They were certainly more intimate than any of the other couples she knew at school. Peggy never talked about it, but then she and Lexi weren't as close as they'd once been.

"Todd agrees with me, don't you?" Jennifer swiveled to face him.

Todd looked uncomfortable, not so much with Jennifer's direct question, but with Peggy and Chad's rumpled appearance.

"Let's just say that if I were Chad, I wouldn't . . ." His voice faded and he looked embarrassed. He shrugged. "It's not my style, that's all."

As Lexi glanced at Todd, she felt a warm rush of pleasure.

"Not my style."

She liked the way he'd said that. Her respect for him inched upward another notch. Todd was a classy guy. She felt he truly respected her—and all of her friends, for that matter.

Sometimes Lexi wondered just how much Chad really respected Peggy —or if Peggy even cared.

Chapter Four

The hallway by the music room was already crowded when Lexi and Jennifer arrived the next morning. The students who had been at the Emerald Tone tryouts the evening before were eagerly pressing their way toward the bulletin board where the roster of the new Emerald Tones was hung.

Lexi clamped her hand across her stomach. "I wish I hadn't eaten breakfast," she moaned to Jennifer. "I'm so nervous I feel sick."

"Butterflies, huh?" Jennifer grinned. "I've got 'em too. Big ones!"

"I think it was a mistake to try out," Lexi said, eyeing the crowd. "There's too much competition for too few spots. I didn't make it, I just know it."

"What about me?" Jennifer piped. "If you don't make it, how could I stand a chance? Your voice is much stronger than mine."

Lexi smiled sheepishly. "Well, maybe instead of standing here convincing ourselves that we failed, we should just try to push our way toward the bulletin board and see if our names are on the list."

Jennifer chuckled. "That would be too easy. Don't you think we need to suffer a little first?"

Lexi shook her head. "I've suffered enough."

"Then what are we waiting for?" Jennifer gave Lexi a shove in the small of her back just as the crowd near the bulletin board parted and Lexi found herself facing the posted list. She read the names aloud.

"Appleton, Bauer, Carter, Epstein, Franks, Garver, Golden, *Golden!*" she squealed. "Jennifer! You made it!"

Quickly she ran her finger down the alphabetically ordered list to the L's. "Lawson, Lawton, Lawrence, *Leighton!*" Lexi squealed. "Jennifer, we *both* made it!"

Heedless of the students standing around her trying to see their names on the list, Lexi flung her arms around Jennifer and they did a gleeful, squealing dance in the middle of the hallway. When one of last year's Emerald Tones began to clap, Lexi realized that she and Jennifer were making royal fools of themselves. Todd sauntered up behind them with an I-told-you-so look on his face.

"We did it, Todd. Isn't that wonderful?"

He nodded cheerfully. "It sure is. I didn't doubt it for a minute. Did you read the note at the bottom of the list?"

Lexi and Jennifer both shook their heads. "Once we saw our names, we didn't look for anything more."

Todd nodded. "I thought so. You're supposed to be in the music room right after school to be measured for your jackets. The rest of us are already outfitted, but you new ET's will have to get your uniforms together quickly. Our first performance will be coming up in a few weeks."

Lexi grabbed Jennifer's hands and gave them a hard squeeze. "Did you hear that? Our first performance."

Jennifer's head was bobbing happily when Binky McNaughton came barreling up beside them. "Congratulations. I just heard the news."

Lexi blinked in surprise. "Then you knew it almost before we did, Bink."

Binky, a tiny, birdlike girl gave a slight shrug. "You know the gossip grapevine in Cedar River High School. News travels at the speed of sound, or faster." She glanced at her watch. "Well, I have to get to class, but I just wanted to tell you how glad I am for both of you."

"Thanks, Binky, we really appreciate it." Lexi put a hand on Binky's thin arm. "You really are a good friend."

Binky bobbed her head in agreement. "Of course I am. See you guys later." Then she tore off down the hall.

Lexi and Jennifer stared at each other for a moment and began to laugh and squeal all over again. When the warning bell for class rang, they realized that they'd better get moving or they'd be late for class.

"Lexi Leighton, Emerald Tone." It looked great doodled across the backs of several of her notebooks, Lexi decided. It had been difficult to concentrate on her classes today.

During her free period Lexi decided to stop at the newspaper office with the roll of film that she'd forgotten in her jacket pocket. Mrs. Drummond had stayed home with a painful case of bursitis. Still, there were a few people working on the newspaper, mostly those involved with layouts.

Minda was seated behind Mrs. Drummond's desk and moaning about the difficulty she was having writing her latest column.

"This is so unbelievably awful!" she complained dramatically to the girl working at the next table. "There is absolutely nothing going on in the school. Nothing! You'd think we lived in a cave or something. How people can stand it here is beyond me. Dull, duller, dullest." Then Minda's blue eyes focused on Lexi.

Minda leaned back in her chair and ran slender fingers through her blond hair as Lexi came by. "Maybe you can help me," she said in a doubtful voice. "As far as I can tell, there's absolutely nothing going on in school this week."

"Sure there is," Lexi answered. "The Emerald Tones just held their tryouts and there's girls' basketball games and the—"

"No, none of that," Minda said in disgust. "That's already old news. You can read it on any bulletin board. I need something really juicy for my gossip column. After all, that's what my readers are used to."

Right, Lexi thought to herself. Minda's readers were used to mean and nasty comments about kids around the school cloaked in just enough secrecy so no one was quite sure who Minda was talking about.

Every time the paper came out with Minda's gossip in it, the students hurried to that page to find out if they could identify Minda's victim of the week. Lexi couldn't understand why Mrs. Drummond allowed it to go on, other than perhaps she really didn't see what Minda was doing. Minda was a clever enough writer to make her column seem bright and witty and funny. It took someone who knew Minda as well as Lexi did to see that her columns could also be very cruel.

"So, Lexi," Minda began, "come on, spill it. Have you heard any juicy stuff lately? Anything that would be great for the column? I'd love to have a real eye-opener this week."

Lexi wanted no part in Minda's "eye-openers." Rather than comment, Lexi merely shook her head, hoping that Minda would consider her uninteresting and begin to ignore her. Lexi had learned the hard way, that it was safest to be ignored by Minda.

Minda, however, was not about to get the hint. Instead, she continued talking about the column with obvious relish. "I really do think the gossip column is the best in the paper. I can say that to you because you and Todd are only working on those dumb photos and aren't writing any other column. Mrs. Drummond made a good decision when she allowed me to alternate the gossip and fashion columns," Minda said, lavishing praise upon herself and her skills. "Everyone tells me that my column is the first one they read."

She paused for a moment and stared hard at Lexi. "That's why you've got to help me. I have to think of something great to put in the paper this week."

"Sorry, Minda," Lexi said. "I'm just not into the new gossip around the school. I don't know a lot of kids. I'm afraid I can't help you."

"That's another reason that you should be reading the column," Minda rejoined, her mind still stuck on her importance to the newspaper. "You're new to Cedar River. You could learn a lot of things about everyone."

Things I don't want to know, Lexi thought to herself. Like who'd reportedly been sent to the administration's office for sleeping in class or who totaled their car the night before when they were at a forbidden party. She switched the little mental switch inside her brain to off, allowing Minda to rattle on about the column without really listening.

Lexi glanced up and was glad to see Egg bolting through the newsroom door. Maybe he could jolt Minda off this persistent quest for juicy gossip.

Then Lexi looked at Egg's face. He wore the sappy, love-sick expression he usually did in Minda's presence. This time, however, when he caught Lexi's warning glance, he rearranged his expression to appear a little more nonchalant.

He'd been burned by Minda in the past. Perhaps he was finally realizing that Minda only respected people she couldn't control. For once Egg was attempting to play it cool where Minda was concerned.

Minda glanced up to see Egg standing in the doorway. She wore an expectant expression, as if she were waiting for Egg to fall all over her as he usually did. The expression changed from expectant to surprised when Egg briefly tipped his head in acknowledgement and mumbled "Hi, Minda," then quickly turned his back to her.

Lexi winked and gave Egg a nod of approval that only he saw. "Play it cool," she mouthed.

Egg nodded. He would do anything that might

cause Minda to notice him, even if it meant ignoring
her. As Egg settled himself in the corner of the room,
working with layout, Minda became restless. She
pushed herself from Mrs. Drummond's desk, picked
up the notebook and pencil that she'd been working
with and moved toward Lexi.

Suddenly Lexi regretted that she hadn't just
turned in the film canister and left the room. Pausing
at the display table to look through a new assortment
of magazines had been a mistake. Minda sidled up
next to her and perched herself on the edge of the
table.

"I hear through the grapevine that Peggy Madison's family is going to London. Is that true?" Minda's eyes narrowed until they were positively catlike.

"Oh? Where'd you hear that?" Lexi parried.

"Just around. I hear Peggy's been bragging about
the fact. She probably thinks she'd be pretty big stuff
because of it." Lexi saw a trace of jealousy in Minda's
expression. Minda hated for anyone but herself to
benefit from any extra attention. "Well, is it true
they're going? That might be something for the column." Minda tapped her front tooth with the tip of
her pen. "Seems like Ms. Madison is having good
luck these days. London. The basketball team.
Pretty soon she'll have to be taken down a notch if
you ask me."

Lexi didn't like the look in Minda's eyes. Her blue
eyes were very cold, calculating and inquisitive. "I
think I'd better be going now, Minda," Lexi murmured. "The bell's going to ring soon." She backed
quickly toward the door before Minda could ask her
anymore questions.

"Are you sure you don't know anything about Peggy's trip to London?" Minda persisted as Lexi exited through the classroom door. "Are you absolutely sure you don't know anything about her?"

Lexi hurried down the tiled hallway, relieved to be away from Minda's appraising stare. Lexi hated that gossip column. Minda's knack for manipulating people must have worked on the unsuspecting Mrs. Drummond. Otherwise she would never let Minda's columns continue.

———

Jennifer had already been measured for her new Emerald Tones' jacket when Lexi arrived at the music room. Mrs. Waverly was adept with the tape measure, and in a few moments both girls were ushered into the hallway with the assurance that the new jackets would arrive before their first performance.

"Are you going right home?" Jennifer wondered.

Lexi looked around. The halls were emptying. Her mother had planned to pick Ben up after school at the Academy and take him with her uptown to make some more inquiries about the juried art show.

"I don't know," Lexi responded. "No one's home right now and won't be for quite awhile. Do you have plans?"

Jennifer tilted her head toward the gymnasium. "I was thinking about stopping and watching the girls' team practice shooting hoops. I think Cedar River is going to have a really good team this year."

"Why don't I come with you?" Lexi suggested. "Mom and Ben will be home late tonight, so it won't matter if I hang around awhile."

"Good enough," Jennifer nodded. "Let's go."

The pair walked through the gymnasium, which smelled of floor wax and sweat, to a spot on the bleachers.

"The coach has the team working hard this afternoon," Lexi observed. Every one of the girls was gleaming with a sheen of sweat and all were huffing and puffing like diesel trains. They were practicing a full court press when Lexi and Jennifer crawled to the topmost seats of the bleachers and settled in to watch.

Lexi's gaze wandered across the court until she saw Peggy. She was normally quick and graceful on the court, but today Peggy was neither. It seemed an effort for her to lift one leg and then the other as she ran. Her movements were listless and apathetic. Perhaps Peggy wasn't feeling well. Her normally creamy skin had a grayish cast and the skin around her eyes seemed taut and drawn.

"What's wrong with Peggy?" Jennifer whispered. "She can't keep up."

"I don't know," Lexi shook her head. "She's not herself, is she?"

"She looks terrible out there," Jennifer commented frankly. "If I were the coach, I'd either tell her to pick it up or get off the floor."

Leave it to Jennifer to be blunt and to the point, Lexi thought. But Jennifer was right. Peggy *was* playing poorly. It was as though she didn't know what to do with the ball or with her hands or feet. While the other girls were glossy with the sheen of perspiration, Peggy had rivulets running down each temple and she kept picking up the tail of her T-shirt and wiping her forehead.

"I think she needs vitamins," Jennifer announced out loud. "Or else she's been staying up too late studying. She looks terrible."

Lexi was silent, her eyes riveted on her friend. Something was desperately wrong with Peggy. Maybe she was getting the flu. She felt Jennifer poke her in the side. "Are you ready to go?"

Lexi shook her head. "I don't think so. I think I'll just wait until basketball practice is over." She paused, "If Peggy isn't feeling well, maybe she'd like some company getting home."

Jennifer nodded. "That's a good idea. I'll wait with you. We never eat until six-thirty anyway."

The girls sat side by side, silently watching the rest of the practice. Obviously the coach hadn't been any happier with Peggy's performance than Jennifer or Lexi had. As the other girls filed off the court into the locker room, he held Peggy back and whatever he was saying was punctuated with emphatic, irate gestures.

Was it her imagination? Lexi wondered, or did Peggy wipe a tear away with the back of her hand?

As Peggy and the coach disappeared into the locker room, Jennifer turned to Lexi, "So, your mom's painting?"

Lexi nodded, "Day and night. I've never seen her so enthusiastic about something. It's as if she's been storing up energy for years and now she's pouring it all out into those paints and brushes. It's almost scary."

Jennifer's nose wrinkled. "Scary? Why do you say that?"

"Mom's been different lately," Lexi stammered,

trying to explain what she didn't truly understand herself. "She's been so bored. She thinks since Ben is so happy at the Academy and I'm making friends at Cedar River High School that we don't need her anymore."

Jennifer stared at Lexi. "Well, that's weird."

Lexi nodded. "I know it is. That's what I tell her, but I can't seem to make her believe that we need her as much as ever. She's convinced herself that we could get along without her."

"Maybe it's a phase," Jennifer said sagely. "Parents are always telling us kids that we're going through them, but I think parents go through phases too. I bet she'll come out of it if you just give her time."

"I hope so," Lexi said, but there was a worried quiver in her voice. "It gives me a really funny feeling to think that my mom isn't satisfied with her life."

Lexi stared across the basketball court and when she began to speak, she was amazed to find herself close to tears. "My mom and dad have never changed ever since I've known them. They've been so . . . steady, like a . . . ."

"Rock?" Jennifer finished for her.

"Yeah, like a rock. And now Mom's turning weird on me."

"Hang in there, Lexi," Jennifer consoled. "Remember? Before my dyslexia was diagnosed I turned weird on you for awhile, too. But I'm straightened out now."

"Well, at least as straightened out as you're going to get," Lexi teased.

Jennifer grinned, "Yeah, I still am a little bit weird, huh?"

"But in a nice sort of way," Lexi amended.

"Well, I'd rather be weird-nice than be like Minda and be weird-nasty."

Lexi winced at that comment. She'd tried to put the thought of Minda and her prying questions into the back of her mind. Still, Lexi reassured herself, there was nothing more that Minda could do to hurt her. Whatever barbs Minda sent out via her gossip column in the *Review*, Lexi would simply ignore. Besides, right now there were much more important things to think about: particularly—what was wrong with Peggy?

Chapter Five

Peggy was the last of the basketball players to make her way out of the showers. She looked pale and grim as she walked slowly toward Lexi and Jennifer as they waited at the bottom of the steps.

"How's it going?" Jennifer asked, oblivious to the somber expression on Peggy's face. "Are you guys going to be ready for the game? You play Cooperville, don't you? Somebody told me that they had a girl who was six-foot-two playing center. How's anybody going to guard her? By wearing stilts?"

As the girls headed home Jennifer rambled on cheerfully about basketball with a dozen questions that Peggy answered as politely and briefly as she could. Only Lexi seemed to notice how strangely she was behaving.

"Here's my corner," Jennifer announced. She turned off the sidewalk and said, "See you tomorrow in school."

Lexi and Peggy waved to her and kept on walking. Lexi sensed that Peggy didn't want to talk. As the two girls moved together, the only sound between

47

them was the small, slapping sound of Peggy's book bag thumping against her back. When they reached the Madison household, Lexi was about to continue her walk when Peggy laid a hand on her arm. "Wait. Can you come in for awhile?"

Lexi blinked in surprise. It had been a long time since Peggy had invited her inside. Usually she and Chad had plans for immediately after supper and Peggy was in a hurry to get her homework done.

Lexi glanced down the street to her own house. It was still dark. "I suppose, for awhile." She followed Peggy through the house and up the stairs to Peggy's bedroom. Lexi glanced around at the cozy clutter and disarray.

"You know," she said, as she dropped her book bag to the bed, "it's been a long time since I've been up here."

Peggy nodded regretfully. "I know. I feel as if I've been ignoring you, Lexi, and I'm sorry."

"There's no need to apologize," Lexi began.

Peggy interrupted her before she could continue. "I know that I haven't been much of a friend since Chad and I started to go steady," Peggy admitted. "But it seems as if there's only so many hours in the day and with basketball and school—"

"It's all right. Really it is." Lexi was uncomfortable. Peggy was so somber tonight. It made Lexi feel very edgy.

In order to escape some of Peggy's intense vibes, Lexi moved idly around the room. First she ran a finger across the top of the desk, then the edge of the nightstand where a stack of books from the public library lay. Lexi hadn't realized that Peggy was such an avid reader, especially of books with titles like *The Human Body*, *Human Sexuality*, and *Science and Self*. There was also a book on human anatomy and a pocket calendar on which Peggy had scribbled with a fine-tipped felt marker.

Lexi absorbed all of this in a second as she made her way to the foot of Peggy's bed. She dropped onto the bed, lay back and cupped her head in her hands.

"So, where's Chad tonight?" she asked.

She regretted the question immediately.

"What you're really asking is why I chose to spend time with you tonight instead of him, isn't it?" Peggy said bluntly.

Lexi shrugged. "Well, you are usually with him night and day."

"His dad had errands he wanted him to run tonight," Peggy said by way of explanation.

Chad's family was quite wealthy, Lexi knew. His father owned a large manufacturing plant on the edge of town. Lexi sometimes saw Chad riding with his father in a huge silver Mercedes Benz.

"I see," she murmured.

Peggy flopped down on the edge of the bed beside Lexi. "Chad told me his father said it's time that Chad start being 'groomed' for the business, whatever that means. He thinks Chad should follow him around on Saturdays and 'get a feel for management.'"

"So Chad is going to follow in his father's footsteps?"

Peggy shrugged. "That's what his father thinks. But Mr. Allen wants Chad to spend about a dozen years in college first. Mr. Allen thinks Chad needs a master's in business. I'm not sure Chad knows what he wants. For one thing, he doesn't like his father dictating his life."

"Why doesn't he tell him that?"

"Because he's a little scared, I guess. His dad can be . . . intimidating."

"I really don't know too much about Chad," Lexi admitted, thinking the life his father had planned for him didn't sound all that appealing. "Has his family lived in Cedar River long?"

"All of his life," Peggy answered. She cupped her chin into her hands and stared at the bedroom wall lined with posters of athletes and ballerinas and kittens. "And Chad's grandfather lived here before them. Mr. Allen considers his family to be founding fathers of Cedar River." She took her index finger and tipped the tip of her nose upward as if to indicate that the Allens were a very snooty family indeed.

"I see. And soon it will be Chad's turn to carry the torch."

Peggy smiled. "That's a funny way of putting it, but I suppose so. His family is all hung up on appearances and doing the right thing. Sometimes it really bugs Chad. But what can he do about it?"

Peggy was silent a moment, as if contemplating what she was about to say next. When she spoke, the words were soft and hesitant. "Chad and his father don't always get along. They've clashed before."

"Over business?" Lexi asked. "Chad seems awfully young to be getting involved in that."

"No, it was over a girl."

Lexi's eyebrow arched so high it disappeared under the fringe of her bangs. "Over a girl? You?"

Peggy shook her head forcefully. "No. It was the girl Chad dated before we met."

"Oh, I see." Lexi hadn't known that there had been another girl in Chad's life.

"She was older," Peggy admitted. "And a lot more experienced, I guess. Chad's father didn't approve of their dating and Chad admits he kept on just because his father didn't like her."

"So he really didn't care for this girl? He just went out with her to make his father angry?" Lexi could see that the question bothered Peggy.

She hesitated a long moment before answering. "That's what I want to think, that Chad didn't really care about her." Her eyes dropped to the comforter on the bed. "I guess I want to think that I'm the first girl that Chad's really ever cared about."

Lexi sat up and curled her legs beneath her in cross-legged fashion and placed the palms of her hands on her knees. She stared intently into her friend's eyes. "Peggy, are you sure it's wise to get so serious about Chad ... about anybody ... right now?"

"You've got Todd," Peggy retorted sharply. "Who are you to ask me about Chad?"

"Todd and I don't have the same kind of relationship that you share with Chad, Peggy, and you know it," Lexi said mildly. "Todd and I are friends. That's the first and most important thing about our relationship. Anyway, you know how my parents are about dating. They'd rather see me going out with groups of friends than going off alone like you and—"

Immediately, Lexi wished she'd bitten her tongue rather than said that. Peggy's eyes flooded with tears and her face crumpled.

"Peggy?" she whispered. "I'm sorry. I didn't mean anything by it."

"You just don't understand," Peggy said with a wail. "I thought you of all people might understand, Lexi, but you don't."

"Give me a chance, Peggy," Lexi pleaded softly. "Give me a chance to understand. Tell me how you feel about Chad. Make me understand."

Peggy scrubbed at her eyes with the backs of her fists. "First Chad's parents, then my parents . . . now even you are giving us a bad time about wanting to spend so much time together alone." She ran her fingers through her thick red hair in frustration. "But you have to understand, Lexi," and her expression was intense and passionate, "I love him."

Lexi considered the statement fully before she spoke.

"Are you sure, Peg? Are you really, truly sure that it's love that you feel for Chad and not . . . something else?"

Peggy glared at her angrily. "Of course I am. What does everyone think I am? An idiot? I know how I feel. I know how I feel when I'm with Chad. Just because I'm not twenty-five years old and on my own doesn't mean that I can't love someone."

"I didn't say that," Lexi defended herself. "I just meant—"

"Oh, I know what you meant all right," Peggy retorted. She paled and the freckles stood out on the bridge of her nose. "You meant that because we're so young, we can't have feelings for each other. We're too young to know what we're really thinking, to know what love is. You think we're play-acting at it. That's it, isn't it?"

Rather than dig herself in any deeper, Lexi settled back to listen. For a few moments, Peggy paced around her room like a nervous lion in a cage too small. When she'd gathered her thoughts, she spoke.

"It's just that Chad and I have grown very close these past weeks," she began. "There's no other way to explain it other than that we love each other. Chad makes me feel so special. Like there's no one else in the world quite like me."

"There *is* no one else quite like you, Peggy," Lexi interjected. "You are special. And you've heard it before. God tells us that."

"There's a big difference between God thinking I'm special and Chad thinking I'm special," Peggy said grimly. "And I feel a whole lot closer to one than the other right now."

"Maybe you're listening to Chad and not listening to God, Peggy," Lexi suggested softly. "But besides that, I agree with both of them. You are special. You're very special to me."

Peggy gave Lexi a weak, teary grin. "Thanks, Lexi. I've always known that I could count on you to say the right thing."

"I don't think I've been doing such a good job today," Lexi pointed out wryly.

Peggy pulled the chair from beneath her desk and sat across from Lexi. "I'm pretty hard to get along with, I know. I've been that way lately. My parents keep threatening to make Chad and me break up or at least force us not to spend so much time together. It's making me really edgy, Lexi. I'm barking at my friends and biting their heads off because I certainly don't dare do it to my parents."

Lexi thought a long moment about what Peggy had said. "Peggy," she began, "have you ever considered that your parents might be right? That maybe you and Chad shouldn't be spending so much time together?"

Lexi thought back to the other evening when Peggy and Chad had come into the Hamburger Shack looking so rumpled and . . . guilty?

"What's the use, Lexi?" Peggy said softly. "I think it's too late already."

"It's never too late," Lexi began and then she paused to stare at her friend. That was a very odd statement. "What do you mean, 'too late,' Peggy?"

Peggy's shoulders slumped and she sighed a deep wrenching sigh. "I haven't been feeling very well lately, Lexi," she admitted finally.

Lexi's smooth brow furrowed into a frown. "I noticed at practice tonight that you weren't quite yourself." Peggy nodded as Lexi continued. "Do you think it's the flu? Maybe you should be taking some vitamins. My mom gave me some vitamins once that really seemed to . . ."

Suddenly Lexi realized that she was babbling into a vacuum. She looked up and stared directly into Peggy's pain-stricken eyes.

"It's not the flu, Lexi, and I'm afraid it is too late. I think I'm pregnant."

Chapter Six

Lexi felt as though she'd been slugged in the stomach with a giant fist. The first words out of her mouth were unsteady.

"Are you sure?"

Peggy shrugged her shoulders helplessly. The tears she'd obviously been fighting flooded her eyes. "Yes. No. I don't know." She gestured toward the stack of books on the nightstand. "I checked some books out of the library. I thought maybe they could help me be sure."

"Did they?"

Peggy made a face. "They list all the signs of pregnancy, but that doesn't tell me anything *positive*."

"What are the signs?"

Peggy flopped into a thickly cushioned easy chair in the corner of the room. She put her feet up on the footstool and ticked off the symptoms on her fingers in the same manner she might have memorized a list of body parts for a biology test.

"A missed period, morning sickness or nausea

during the day, going to the bathroom a lot, tender breasts, mood swings."

"And have you had any of that?"

"All of the above," Peggy said grimly. "Sometimes I think I'm absolutely going to die first hour in the morning at school. I want to throw up, but then everybody would guess." She stared gloomily out the window. "I think dying would be easier than this."

"Stop it!" Lexi said sharply.

An expression of regret washed over her features. "I didn't mean it, Lexi. It's just that . . ." She sighed and rubbed the tears from her eyes. "Chad and I never should have—" She broke off abruptly, a mottled red stain growing across her neck and face.

"Does Chad know?"

Peggy shook her head. "I think he might suspect. I haven't wanted to do . . . it . . . lately. I'm sure he suspects that something is wrong." She threw her head against the back of the chair. "I don't know if it's occurred to him that this could have happened."

"You've got to tell him."

"No."

Lexi's eyes grew wide. "No? Why not?"

"Not until I'm sure, Lexi. What if this was just a false alarm? Why get Chad all upset?"

"Because he's in this too. He's every bit as responsible for this as you are." Lexi paused a moment before adding, "It's his baby too, Peggy."

Peggy's eyes fluttered and closed. "Don't say that word."

"Don't say 'baby?' But that's what it is, Peggy. A baby. A brand new little soul you and Chad might have started. No matter what I call it, that's what it is."

Peggy put her hands over her ears. "Stop it! Maybe it's all a big mistake! Maybe I've got the flu." Her eyes opened, a spark of hope flickering in them. "I've probably got the flu! I'll bet I've been worrying for nothing . . ."

"The flu doesn't stop your period, Peggy." Lexi's voice was soft and sorry, but Peggy was trying very hard to deny what was most likely the truth.

Peggy paled.

"You've got to find out for sure if you're pregnant or not," Lexi said firmly. "If you are, it's not going to go away, and if you aren't, you're torturing yourself unnecessarily."

"I wanted to get one of those home pregnancy tests," Peggy admitted.

"Why didn't you?"

"And take a chance on my parents finding out I bought one? Are you kidding? That's why Chad and I didn't use any . . . protection. . . . He thought his parents might somehow find out what he was buying."

Lexi sagged against the foot of the bed. "If you're pregnant, *everybody* is going to know what you've been doing, Peggy."

Peggy's face was as white as the pillowcases and fluffy comforter across her bed. Her eyes, red-rimmed and swollen, were like two painful pricks of light in her face. "What am I going to do, Lexi?"

Lexi could feel the weight of Peggy's problems shifting to her shoulders. There was a new burden on her heart as well. It was as clear to Lexi as if God had stepped into the room and given her a verbal command to help Peggy. Lexi was to help her friend get through this. But how? God would have to tell her.

What do I do, Father? Lexi pleaded silently as she stared at her friend. *I don't know anything about this! I'm no good at helping a pregnant teenager! Why me?*

Why not you? The thought sprang into her mind with such suddenness that Lexi blinked in surprise.

Why not me? If God thought she could help Peggy through this, she could—with His guidance, of course.

Lexi was silent a moment longer, sorting her thoughts. When she spoke, it was with new authority. "You've got to tell your parents."

"I can't, Lexi. I just can't."

"You have to."

"They'll kill me, Lexi. You know how they are. Appearances are very important to them. The last thing they want is a pregnant teenager."

"You can't say that for sure. They might surprise you."

Peggy shook her head stubbornly. "No. I know them too well. All I'd do is embarrass them. My mother will say, 'I thought we raised you better than that!' and my father will . . ." Peggy shuddered. "I just can't tell them."

"Have you seen a doctor?"

"Are you kidding? My family doctor would be on the phone to my parents in two minutes. And where would I get the money to pay for another one?"

Lexi felt as though she were caught in a circular maze with no exit.

"You've simply got to tell someone, Peggy. Someone who can help you."

"No one can help me." Peggy sank lower into the chair and folded her hands morosely over her still-flat stomach. "No one."

Lexi knew this wasn't the time to talk about how God could help Peggy. First she had to get Peggy to help herself.

"If you don't tell your parents, I will."

Peggy sat bolt upright in the chair. "You wouldn't!"

"I would. I'd go with you to your parents and if you couldn't bring yourself to talk, I'd do the talking for you." Lexi's voice trembled. "I'd be scared, Peggy, but I'd do it. Your parents have to know. If you are pregnant and ignore it, they'll find out anyway. Maybe there's something you should be doing—eating special food, taking vitamins or something. You have to get someone to help you!"

"But it could be the flu. If I tell them and then I'm not pregnant, they'll make me stop seeing Chad."

"It seems to me you've seen too much of him already." Peggy gave her an icy look. Then her expression brightened. "You can help me get a pregnancy test!"

"Me?" Lexi squeaked.

"Yes, you. If it's positive, I'll tell my parents and Chad. If it's not"—she spread her hands wide—"then everything will be all right!"

Lexi hardly agreed with that sentiment. Everything *wouldn't* be all right. Even if Peggy weren't pregnant, she and Chad were going to have to make some decisions about what they'd been doing and the potential consequences. But for now, the most important thing was to convince Peggy to get some help.

"I don't know how I could help you, Peggy."

"Just go with me to that mall on Hampton. Not many people we know shop over there. I can probably get into and out of a drugstore without being seen. You can act as my lookout just in case someone familiar comes by."

"But I haven't lived here very long. How will I know your family's friends?"

"You'll be fine. Please?"

Lexi sighed. This sounded hair-brained to her, but what could she do? If the kit would force Peggy into talking to her parents, then she would have to help Peggy get the test.

"I suppose, but I don't like it."

Peggy looked a little more hopeful. "It's probably all for nothing, Lexi. I'll bet I have the flu."

"How long have you been sick to your stomach?"

"About a month."

"The flu doesn't last a month, Peggy." Lexi's words seemed to fly over Peggy's head.

Peggy leapt from the chair and paced the room, intent on planning the cloak and dagger mission that would gain her the pregnancy test kit. Again Lexi admired Peggy's athletic strength. Would this mean Peggy would have to quit basketball too? Lexi sighed as she stood up. She had a hunch that Peggy hadn't yet fully realized what a high price she might have to pay for taking life's events out of God's planned order.

———

Their shopping trip was to take place on Saturday morning. Lexi dragged herself unenthusiastically out of bed when the alarm rang. She was to meet Peggy at nine o'clock sharp. The mall opened at nine-thirty and Peggy thought that if they were at the drugstore early, there would be fewer people to run into.

She dressed in jeans and an unappealing beige sweater. Peggy also had the idea that if they looked nondescript, it might help. Lexi felt this was a childish game to be playing over anything as important as a new life, but Peggy was adamant—and it was Peggy's future at stake, not Lexi's.

"My, but you're up early," Mrs. Leighton commented. She was already at the kitchen table reading the morning paper and sipping a cup of coffee. Her hair was rumpled and she still wore her pale blue bathrobe. "If I'd known, I would have made pancakes. Do you want me to mix some up?"

"No thanks. Toast is fine."

"Are you sure? I haven't got anything else to do today. I'd be glad to make you anything. A bagel? Some fresh-squeezed orange juice?"

Lexi held up a hand to make her mother stop. The more bored her mother seemed around the house, the more food she cooked.

Mrs. Leighton stopped fussing long enough to put her hands on her hips and stare at her daughter. "You look serious. Something troubling you? Want to talk?"

Leave it to her mother to see right through her, Lexi thought.

"I'm going shopping with Peggy."

"That's nice. I'm glad to see you girls spending time together again." Mrs. Leighton frowned. "When she started seeing Chad, it seemed she didn't have much time for you. I think her parents made a big mistake allowing that relationship to get too serious too soon."

"Are you ready for your art show?" Lexi asked, hoping to change to a more comfortable subject.

Mrs. Leighton nodded. "It's been fun to get back to my painting in a serious way, but I still feel like it's a rather shallow way to spend my time. I don't feel as if I'm *helping* anyone."

"You're giving people the pleasure of seeing your painting," Lexi pointed out.

Mrs. Leighton smiled. "You flatter me, darling, but thank you. That makes me feel better."

Lexi shoved the last of her toast into her mouth. "I've got to go. Peggy will be waiting for me." Grabbing her jacket, Lexi darted out of the kitchen before her mother could ask any more questions.

Peggy was already outside, coming up the sidewalk. "Hurry up or we'll miss the bus."

Lexi reluctantly picked up her pace. "You don't look sick this morning," she commented.

Peggy nodded. "I feel pretty good if I can get out of the house without eating breakfast. Mom is always nagging at me to eat something. Sometimes I have to put my toast in my backpack and dump it in the girls' bathroom at school."

The two girls were silent for most of the bus ride, both lost in their own thoughts. Lexi had been awake several times in the night thinking about Peggy. Each time, she'd prayed for her friend until sleep overtook her again.

The ride seemed endless. The bus stopped at every corner to pick up and release passengers. Peggy looked rather green by the time they got off at the mall.

"Come on, if we hurry we can be in and out of the Drug Mart before anyone has a chance to see us."

Lexi followed several steps behind her friend down the nearly empty hall. Peggy stationed her between a potted palm and a U.S. Post Office stamp dispenser.

"You're my look-out. If you see anyone coming that I know, come in and warn me." With that, Peggy disappeared into the store.

Lexi felt rather silly standing there with nothing to do but stare at the people staring at her. To make herself appear occupied, she dug in her pocket for change to buy a stamp. She could see Peggy coming toward her from the back of the store as she bent to make her little purchase.

With her back turned, she didn't see Minda Hannaford and Tressa Williams coming down the hall until it was too late.

"Writing letters, Lexi?"

Lexi straightened with a start, the little cardboard folder containing her stamp crushed in her hand.

"Minda! Tressa! Hello." Lexi caught the look of panic on Peggy's face but it was too late; they'd both been seen.

"Peggy's shopping too, I see." Minda smiled sweetly as her eyes darted to Peggy's package.

Lexi could never tell quite what Minda was up to. Had she seen from which department of the pharmacy Peggy had come? Or was their own guilt making them think they had their secret plans written all over their faces?

"Hullo Minda, Tressa," Peggy muttered. Then she pulled at Lexi's sleeve. "I promised Mom I'd be back early. We'd better get our shopping done."

Lexi nodded dully. She'd been a lousy look-out and she knew she was terrible at keeping her emotions from showing in her face. She wished she'd stayed home in bed.

"Bye."

"Bye."

The four parted. Peggy whistled into Lexi's ear. "Why didn't you tell me they were coming down the hall?"

"I was buying a postage stamp."

"A stamp? They could have caught us!"

"I thought it would look less suspicious than pretending to be a potted plant."

Peggy shuddered. "Well, that was close, but I got it."

Lexi nodded gloomily and was silent. She didn't have the heart to tell Peggy that as they'd walked away from Drug Mart, Lexi'd turned back to see where Minda and Tressa had gone. They'd gone directly into the drugstore, to the counter from which Peggy had just come.

Chapter Seven

The rest of the weekend dragged with dreadful slowness. Lexi tried to call the Madison household several times, but the only response she received was that of their answering machine.

Rather than risk giving away her distress over Peggy's predicament, Lexi chose to stay home with her family. Spending time with perceptive Todd or inquisitive Binky would have been dangerous for her. She was longing to talk to someone, but Peggy had sworn her to secrecy.

Ben, however, was delighted to have his big sister all to himself. Lexi played a dozen games of "Uncle Wiggley," two dozen games of checkers, and read to Ben from a large stack of books he'd been collecting for just such an occasion.

On Sunday afternoon the entire family went to view the juried art show in which Mrs. Leighton had entered her paintings.

By Monday morning, Lexi felt as though she were going to burst—from curiosity, from anticipation, and from just plain nervous tension.

She looked for Peggy as she entered the high school. Their lockers were only a few feet apart. Lexi hoped to have a minute alone with her friend to find out what the results of the test had been. But that was not to be. When Lexi finally saw Peggy, she was engulfed in a group of students all pressing toward their lockers.

Peggy appeared pale and quiet as the crowd jostled her. Listlessly she pushed her way forward and swung open her locker door.

Lexi bit at her lower lip. There was no way they could talk here. Whatever news Peggy had to tell her would have to wait.

Just as Lexi turned toward her classroom, she heard Jerry Randall's voice booming through the hallway.

"My parents should be here any time now. They could be at my aunt and uncle's tonight, for all I know. When my folks come home, you should see all the stuff they bring for me! Last time they brought my stereo system and a leather jacket. The time before, it was a . . ."

Lexi tuned out Jerry's chatter. The closer it came to the time of his parents' arrival, the more he was bragging about it. It was almost pitiful, really. No one seemed to care about Jerry's parents but Jerry himself, yet he persisted in announcing to the world that they were arriving.

Of course, Lexi mused, if her parents left her in the care of an aunt and uncle and were absent for months at a time, maybe she'd behave just as Jerry was today.

"Emerald Tones. After school. Be there!" Jennifer

barked with mock gruffness as they passed in the hallway. "Rehearsal!"

Lexi gave a gusty little sigh of frustration. There wasn't going to be a single chance to talk to Peggy all day.

She couldn't keep her mind on the music at practice. All Lexi could think about was Peggy and what the test had shown. Lexi knew absolutely nothing about at-home pregnancy tests, but according to the directions on the box, if Peggy had done it correctly she should know something by now. Unfortunately, the test box said that a negative result could be wrong and still advised a visit to the doctor.

If only Peggy weren't so adamant about not telling her parents! It was beginning to frighten Lexi. Peggy needed more help than Lexi alone could offer. She could pray, but Peggy needed her parents—to pay clinic bills, to make future plans, to . . .

It was overwhelming. If Peggy was pregnant, her entire life would be unalterably changed.

Lexi gave herself a mental shake. Maybe Peggy wasn't pregnant. There was no use worrying until she had all the facts.

———

The Emerald Tones rehearsal ran nearly thirty minutes longer than expected. Todd caught up to Lexi at the door to the music room.

"Need a ride home? I'm going right away. Mom asked me to do some errands for her and I'm running late."

"No thanks. I think I'll walk. Your errands will go faster if you don't have to bother with me." Lexi didn't mention that her plan was to waylay Peggy on the way out of basketball practice.

"Are you sure? I don't mind."

"I know you don't, Todd. Thanks, but I'd really like the exercise today."

"Okay. See you tomorrow." He dipped his blond head and gave her a glimpse of his most appealing smile.

Lexi was still staring after him when Jennifer approached her.

"I'm late! My mother is going to have a fit! I promised I'd make supper tonight and I forgot to tell her to take out any meat and now it's late and . . . are you walking with me?"

Lexi smiled at Jennifer's breathlessness. "It's so late that I think I'll wait for Peggy—if that's all right with you."

Jennifer studied Lexi's face. "You and Peggy seem to be spending more time together lately—without Chad."

Lexi nodded. "I'm trying to. I think she needs some girl friends as well as a boyfriend."

Jennifer nodded. "I agree. She and Chad are nauseating to watch. He has his hands all over her. Maybe you can talk some sense into her. She confides in you." Jennifer's expression softened. "You are probably the best listener I've ever met. You were always there for me when I needed you."

Lexi felt a rush of affection for her friend. Jennifer was not usually so open about her emotions. "And I know you'll be around for me."

"I hope so," Jennifer said intently. Then she slipped into her usual blunt role. "Meanwhile, do your best to talk some sense into Peggy. It's sickening to see them smooching in the school halls. Call me later."

"Right."

Jennifer's departure left Lexi alone in the hallway. She could hear pounding footsteps in the gymnasium and knew that basketball practice was in progress. Lexi slipped inside to watch.

Peggy was sitting on the sidelines, her legs sprawled in front of her and leaning backward against the bleachers. Her eyes were closed and she looked very pale. Alarmed, Lexi hurried to her side.

"Are you okay?"

Peggy's eyes fluttered open. "Fine. I got bumped in the head and Coach said to sit out until my vision cleared."

Lexi glanced at the playing floor. "Should I leave? Maybe I shouldn't be talking to you during practice."

"It's okay. I'm not going to play for awhile anyway." Peggy patted the bleacher next to her. "Sit down."

Lexi had barely settled herself when Peggy announced tonelessly. "I'm pregnant. It's for sure."

Lexi swallowed hard. Her eyes went directly to Peggy's sweat-covered face. Instead of the flushed pink coloring of the rest of the players, Peggy looked gray and drained. "The test was positive?"

"Positive. No if's, and's, or maybe's. I'm pregnant." Peggy rubbed a hand wonderingly across her stomach. "I can hardly believe it."

"Peggy, should you be . . . I mean, maybe it would be better if you didn't . . . Couldn't it be dangerous or something to . . ." Lexi found herself stammering.

"To what?"

"To be playing basketball. If you're carrying a baby, maybe you'd better be careful. . . ." Lexi stopped short when she saw the desperate expression in Peggy's eyes. When Peggy spoke, her words and tone were harsh and bitter.

"Are you kidding? Basketball is probably the most important thing in my life next to Chad! I'm not going to quit playing basketball!" She paused for a long moment. When she spoke again, Lexi could hear the desperation in her voice, "Maybe if I play hard enough, I'll lose it."

"Peggy!"

"Well, what do you expect me to do? Be happy? I'm sixteen years old! I don't want a baby!"

"Maybe you should have thought of that before now."

Lexi was sorry the moment the words left her lips. She clapped her hands across her mouth, but there was no way to draw back the hurt—or truth—in her words.

Suddenly Peggy jumped to her feet. She stumbled a little but managed to catch herself. Silently, she returned to the playing floor. Without a backward look, Lexi left the gymnasium. She hadn't meant to be so brutally frank with Peggy, but maybe that's what she needed right now. Somehow she had to be convinced that her pregnancy wasn't an issue she could keep ignoring. A baby wasn't something she could wish away.

Lexi stood in the hallway with her hands over her eyes. *Now what?*

"Are you okay?"

When Lexi opened her eyes, Jerry Randall was peering into them. His forehead was furrowed with concern.

"Oh! Jerry! Yeah, I'm fine. It's just that—"

"Are you going to pass out or something?"

Lexi smiled weakly. "No. I've just got something on my mind, that's all."

"Oh, okay. Just so you aren't sick or anything."

She gave him an appraising glance. Jerry had come a long way from the rude boy she'd met when she'd first moved to Cedar River. "Thanks for being concerned. It's just been one of 'those' days."

"Yeah?" Jerry huffed. "Tell me about it. I thought it would never end!"

"Tests?"

"No. It's just that my parents are coming soon and I wish they'd hurry up and get here."

"Has it been a long time since you've seen them?"

"Too long." His expression turned serious. "I haven't seen them since I had the car accident and nearly killed your brother."

Lexi put her hand on Jerry's arm and gave a comforting squeeze. That accident was thankfully buried in the past for her family even though Jerry still suffered for what he'd almost done.

"Ben's fine, Jerry. And I doubt you'll ever do anything like that again."

His shoulders sagged. "I hope my parents don't ask too many questions about that night. I don't want this visit ruined."

His words and voice were so plaintive that Lexi felt sorry for him. What must it be like to have parents that flew into your life for a visit and then flew out again?

As she trudged home from school, dozens of questions swirled through Lexi's mind. And of all the questions that nagged at her, those about Peggy were the most difficult to answer.

After saying hello to her mother, who was up to her elbows in a canvas-stretching project, Lexi went directly to her room. When she had questions, there was one place that always seemed to hold an answer.

She flicked on her lamp, curled onto the edge of the bed and picked up her Bible.

How was she supposed to discover what God had to say about teenage pregnancy? Lexi wondered. She couldn't really trot downstairs and ask her mother without setting off a dozen alarms!

Because she didn't know where to begin her search, Lexi simply turned to one of her favorite books of the Bible, the Psalms. If nothing else, the verses might have a calming effect on her.

She'd read for nearly an hour when the words seemed to leap off the page.

> For thou didst form my inward parts,
> thou didst knit me together in my
>   mother's womb.
> I praise thee, for thou art fearful and
>   wonderful.
> Wonderful are thy works!
> Thou knowest me right well;
>   my frame was not hidden from thee.
> When I was being made in secret,
> intricately wrought in the depths of
>   the earth.
> Thy eyes beheld my unformed substance;

> in the book they were written,
> every one of them, the days that
> were formed for me,
> When as yet there were none of them.

Lexi stared at the passage for a long time. Her room was so silent that the mild hum of the electric clock on her bedside stand seemed like a roar.

The words were not a teenager's words, that was obvious, but it was the message she'd been looking for. Lexi took a pen and notebook from the drawer of the night stand and began to write.

> You made me, God, intestines and all.
> You put me together, like a jigsaw puzzle,
> right there in my mother's womb.
> And it was a pretty miraculous thing
> You did, too! But then, everything
> You do is pretty awesome.
> You know me better than I know myself.
> I've never been out of Your sight and
> there's nowhere in the world I
> can hide from You.
> You knew my mom was pregnant before
> she or Dad did and knew all
> about my life before I'd even
> lived at all.
> Wow!

Lexi stared at her paraphrase for a long time. If she'd gotten it right, if Psalm 139 was saying what she thought it was, then Peggy and Chad's baby was known to God too—and had been from the very first moment. God was knitting that baby together inside of Peggy just as He had done for every other being in the world.

Lexi sagged against the bed. This made it all so much more real and worrisome. Did Peggy and Chad even realize what a chain of events they'd set in motion?

———

Lexi was silent all through supper, grateful for Ben's cheerful chatter and her mother's latest reports on the progress of her painting. After the dishes were dried and put away, Lexi hurried back to her room.

With renewed purpose, she dialed the telephone.

"Hello. Madisons'."

"Peggy?"

"What do you want?" Peggy's voice was flat and toneless.

"Did you tell them?"

"No."

"When are—"

"But I told Chad."

The silence of the line hummed between them.

"And?"

"He's scared, Lexi." Peggy's voice cracked. "Scared as me."

"Now what?"

"I'm not sure. We're going to have to tell our parents soon. Chad said that he didn't expect—" She broke off.

"Expect what?"

"Expect me to get pregnant."

"That's pretty naive, considering what you had to be doing," Lexi said bluntly.

She could hear Peggy sighing across the line.

"I know, but his other girl friend . . ."

"The one who was older than he?"

"She must have taken care of . . . you know . . ."

"Birth control?" Lexi groaned. "Peggy, you know better! Why did you ever let things go that far? You know what we've talked about in church and—"

"I know. You don't have to remind me. Sometimes I feel so eaten up with guilt that I want to die! But I didn't *mean* to let anything happen! Chad was more experienced than I, but I thought I could handle it. And I *do* love him! It seemed all right to be parking somewhere out of the way and talking—"

"Obviously it was more than talking."

"Not at first. At first it was just . . . nice. Then one thing led to another and . . ."

Lexi remained silent. She'd heard the lecture from her parents on the dangers of too much togetherness for a boy and girl. She guessed that this was a prime example of what could happen. It was too bad for Chad and Peggy's sake that parents were usually so right. . . . It was Peggy who brought up the next troublesome subject.

"I tried to talk to Rita Leonard today."

Rita? Lexi tried to fix a picture of the girl in her mind. "That tall blond who has a locker near yours?"

"That's the one. She's a Hi-Five."

"Of course." Everyone who seemed aloof and unfriendly was a Hi-Five. Rita wore thick, black eyemakeup and blood-red lipstick. She usually looked like a little girl who'd gone too heavy on her mother's makeup.

"I heard once that Rita had an abortion."

"Oh?" Lexi murmured cautiously.

"I thought maybe I'd get a chance to talk to her."

"About what?"

"Get real, Lexi. What else? I'd be a fool not to check it out."

"You don't want to have an abortion, Peggy!"

"Don't I? I'm not so sure what I want anymore."

"You aren't thinking clearly, that's all. Once you tell your parents, they'll help to think this thing through—"

"It will hurt them so much, Lexi!" Peggy sounded as if she was ready to cry. "I can't even imagine how disappointed they're going to be. Mom is always telling me how proud she is of what I've accomplished in school and Dad . . ." She stopped abruptly. "If I have an abortion, maybe they won't have to know . . ."

Lexi grabbed for her Bible and the notebook on the bed. "Will you listen to something I read, Peggy? Please?"

She read the psalm, all twenty-four verses, and then the simple paraphrase she'd created. Peggy was silent. When Lexi finished, she asked, "You understand what it says, don't you, Peggy? That we're so important to God that He knows all about us from the minute we're conceived until the minute we—"

"If I caught Rita right after school, maybe I could bring up the subject of abortion—like I saw a TV program on it or something. Maybe that's what I'll do. I heard that she doesn't mind talking about it if there aren't any guys around. It would be worth it, even if I had to skip basketball practice. I mean, who else can I ask about something like that?"

It was as though Peggy hadn't heard a single word Lexi had said. Lexi might as well have been talking to the wall.

rved with a smile as Lexi slid into the car next
im. Egg and Binky were in the backseat, having
isy argument about tennis shoes.

Just glad to get out of the house, that's all."
odd glanced at her sharply and his observant
eyes seemed to read into her very soul. "Trou-
"

Not really. Not at my house, at least."
exi was grateful that Todd knew when to ask
tions and when to remain silent. She wanted
erately to talk about this situation with him, but
as Peggy's secret and not Lexi's to tell. Egg and
y were still carrying on when they arrived at
ealth club.

You think you're so smart! I'll bet you don't even
how to play racquetball!" Binky accused sourly
gg tried to list the fundamentals of the game for
ister.

gg's face got red and splotchy. Lexi was expect-
to see steam coming out his ears any moment
Todd stepped in to calm things down.

Why don't Binky and I use the court for awhile
Egg? I can show her a few shots and get her
ainted with the feel of the racquet before we try
ing a game. You and Lexi can use the treadmill
ft weights to warm up. How about that?"

Fine with me," Egg blustered. "I'm not sure why
n thought I could teach Binky this game. She
r believes anything I say."

If you wouldn't tease her so much, she'd probably
t you more," Todd pointed out cheerfully.

gg gave a wicked grin. "Oh, yeah."
exi looped her hand around Egg's scrawny el-

"Peggy," she began again, "at least tell your parents. They're the ones you should be talking to, not Rita Leonard. Please tell your parents!"

Peggy's final words sent a chill down Lexi's spine. "Who knows? Maybe I won't have to."

Chapter Eight

The weekend came and Peggy had
tacted Lexi.

When Binky called and suggested
Lexi accompany Egg and Todd to the
court, Lexi grabbed the opportunity—
distract her from thoughts of Peggy and

"Egg said he and Todd would teach
Do you need a lesson too?"

"My father and I have played," Lexi
I'm not exactly a beginner. I could use
though."

"Okay. Todd is coming in about fifte
We'll be at your house after that."

Lexi threw a pair of shorts and a t
her bag and dug a racquet out of her fat
Maybe whacking away at one of thos
balls would release some of the pent-up
concern about Peggy was creating. She
on the front steps when Todd's old '49
pulled up in front of the house.

"You must be anxious to play racq

bow. "Come on. First one to the weight room gets her choice of machines."

"You mean *his* choice," Egg retorted and plunged ahead.

Lexi had put three kilometers on the ski machine when Todd came loping down the stairs. "Your turn Eggo, my man. Your sister wants to take you on."

"You're kidding, right?" Egg said in disbelief. Still, he swung off the slantboard and headed for the courts. "She wants to be creamed by me. The girl is a glutton for punishment."

As Egg disappeared, Lexi asked, "How was Binky's first lesson?"

Todd chuckled. "The girl is a natural. She'll run circles around Egg in no time. She wants to show off."

They were both laughing when Jerry Randall came storming into the weight room. His eyes were cloudy and his expression black. Without saying hello, he moved toward the weights. Silently, he began to do arm curls until his face was red and his cheeks were puffed out like those of a gopher.

When he stopped to rest, Todd inquired calmly, "Bad day, Jerry?"

"None of your business."

"I don't know about that. Lexi and I were here first."

Jerry scowled. "I need to blow off some steam. Do you mind?"

Todd shrugged. "I thought your parents were here. Why aren't you home with them?"

Jerry's scowl deepened. "I couldn't take any more."

Lexi felt a nudge of surprise. "But you were so anxious for them to come!"

"Yeah, but the feeling wasn't mutual."

Lexi and Todd exchanged a puzzled glance. Todd's next question was cautious. "You mean they didn't want to be here?"

"Not any longer than necessary. They're just 'checking in' to see if I'm behaving." Jerry's bullish bravado seemed to dissolve before their eyes. He lay on the weight bench, his body slack. The angry mask was replaced by a look of miserable frustration. "I thought they'd stay this time."

"What about their jobs?"

Jerry swung his feet to the floor and returned Todd's steady gaze. "What about *me*? Far as I can tell, they'd be happier if I'd never been born!"

"Jerry, I—"

"They came home to see if I'd gotten into any more trouble. They wanted to make sure I wasn't giving my aunt and uncle too many headaches, that's all." Jerry's tone was hurt and bitter. "Maybe I *should* give them a few problems if that's what they're looking for."

Todd moved quietly toward Jerry. "I think you'd better tell them how you feel. Maybe they don't realize how hard it is on you to live without them."

"What makes you think they'd listen?"

"They came to check on you. The least you can do is tell them what's going on." Todd was thoughtful for a moment, then added, "It's better to tell them than to jump angrily behind the wheel of a car and have another accident."

At that, Jerry spun around on the toe of his tennis shoe and left the room.

Todd gave a low whistle beneath his breath as they watched him leave. "There goes one guy who really needs his parents." Lexi nodded. She knew of another person who needed her parents just as much. The rest of the afternoon Lexi could concentrate on nothing but Peggy.

———

It was late Sunday evening when the telephone rang. Intuitively, Lexi knew who was calling.

"Lexi? Can we talk?"

"My parents are in the other room if that's what you mean."

"Mine just went out for a drive. They asked me if I wanted to come and I told them I had homework."

"Do you?"

"Of course! What do you think I'd do, lie to . . ." Peggy's voice faded.

"Have you told them about the baby?"

"Don't call it a baby, Lexi. It's a fetus—"

"Then you haven't told them."

"I just couldn't—"

"Then that's as good as lying to them, Peg! Don't you see?"

There was a long silence on the other end of the line. When Peggy began to speak, her voice was quavery.

"Listen, could you come over for awhile? I really need to talk to somebody."

Lexi glanced at her watch. "For a little while. Hang on. I'll be right there."

The only light on in the Madison household was a small reading lamp in the living room. Peggy was curled on the window seat on the far side of the room, bathed in shadows. Having let herself in, Lexi walked silently across the floor to sit by her friend.

"I talked to Rita about her abortion," Peggy blurted.

"Did you tell her you were—"

"Are you kidding? I just made sure the subject came up in a roundabout way and then started asking questions. I don't think she suspected anything. She's talked to others about it."

Lexi had a sick feeling in the pit of her stomach. She couldn't quit thinking about that paraphrase she'd written of Psalm 139. *You made me, God, intestines and all. You put me together, like a jigsaw puzzle, right there in my mother's womb.*

"What did she say?"

Peggy looked a little green even in the dim light. "She said it was scary, but it was over pretty fast. She had a D & C."

Lexi looked blank.

"She said that meant dilation and curettage. It's scraping the inside of your womb so that there's . . . nothing . . . there anymore." Peggy's voice lowered. "I guess there are other ways too. Rita called it a suction abortion. Sort of like vacuuming out your insides, I guess."

"Peggy," Lexi began, but Peggy wouldn't let her continue.

Voice artificially bright, Peggy kept talking. "Rita says sometimes girls wait too long and then it's harder to do. The doctor can make you go into labor and deliver the baby or else you can have surgery. I wouldn't want to wait that long. It would be easier if—"

"Are you listening to yourself?" Lexi blurted. "There's *nothing* easy about what you're talking about! You can't make decisions like this without talking to your parents! And didn't you listen to *anything* I said about what's in the Psalms? Have you thought about what it is God might want you to do?"

"But what about what *I* want to do?" Peggy's face was contorted with distress. "What else *can* I do? I'm too young to have a baby! It would ruin everything for me! It's already ruining things between me and Chad." Peggy clamped a hand over her lips as if that bit of information was not meant to come out.

"You and Chad are having trouble?"

Peggy's shoulders slumped even farther. "He's edgy, that's all. I think he's mad because I let this happen."

Lexi gave a snort. "And where was he? Doesn't he think he has any responsibility for this?"

"He says we can get married, but we're not even done with high school yet! Chad wants to go to college." Her voice broke and she whispered, "I did too."

Lexi remained silent as Peggy rose and began to pace around the darkened room. She was talking more to herself than to Lexi.

"Coach told me on Friday that I could be a starter for the team for sure. I'm the youngest one on varsity. It's a real honor and now . . ." She rubbed ruefully at her stomach. "I wish I didn't feel so sick all the time. I'm afraid someone will find out and I'll be kicked off the team without ever getting a chance to show anyone how good I could be."

Peggy drifted to the couch and sat down. "Nobody's ever going to know what I'm good at—maybe not even me. How am I supposed to make plans for college now? Maybe all I'm good at is making a mess of things." Her eyes flooded with tears. "I've really done that, Lexi."

A harsh, unlovely laugh escaped her. "My family is still talking about going to London so my dad can do research. I think it would be the most wonderful place in the world to visit. But now..." Peggy slammed her fist into the cushiony soft pillows on the davenport. "This baby has ruined my life!"

"I'm not sure it's the baby you should be angry with, Peggy," Lexi said softly.

Peggy's face crumpled. "I know. It didn't ask to exist. But I didn't ask it to exist either!"

"In a way you did," Lexi pointed out. "You and Chad made some choices."

"Great choices," Peggy said bitterly. "What we were doing seemed okay at the time. It was romantic, I guess. I never thought about what might happen until *after* we'd ..." Her voice faded. "And then it was too late and I'd put it out of my mind until the next time ..."

"Talk to your parents, Peggy. Please?" Lexi pleaded. "I can't help you with this. I've been praying and reading the Bible, but you don't seem to want to listen to me." Lexi gave a weak smile. "Actually, I don't blame you. I've probably been pretty hard on you."

Peggy smiled weakly. "It's okay. I know how strong your faith is, Lexi, and I did listen to what you said even though it might not have seemed that way. It's just that I'm not old enough or smart enough to have this baby, Lexi. I'm too young! What else can I do?"

"Peggy," she began again, "at least tell your parents. They're the ones you should be talking to, not Rita Leonard. Please tell your parents!"

Peggy's final words sent a chill down Lexi's spine. "Who knows? Maybe I won't have to."

Chapter Eight

The weekend came and Peggy had not yet contacted Lexi.

When Binky called and suggested that she and Lexi accompany Egg and Todd to the racquetball court, Lexi grabbed the opportunity—anything to distract her from thoughts of Peggy and her problem.

"Egg said he and Todd would teach me to play. Do you need a lesson too?"

"My father and I have played," Lexi admitted, "so I'm not exactly a beginner. I could use the practice though."

"Okay. Todd is coming in about fifteen minutes. We'll be at your house after that."

Lexi threw a pair of shorts and a tee-shirt into her bag and dug a racquet out of her father's closet. Maybe whacking away at one of those little blue balls would release some of the pent-up energy her concern about Peggy was creating. She was waiting on the front steps when Todd's old '49 Ford Coupe pulled up in front of the house.

"You must be anxious to play racquetball," he

observed with a smile as Lexi slid into the car next to him. Egg and Binky were in the backseat, having a noisy argument about tennis shoes.

"Just glad to get out of the house, that's all."

Todd glanced at her sharply and his observant blue eyes seemed to read into her very soul. "Trouble?"

"Not really. Not at my house, at least."

Lexi was grateful that Todd knew when to ask questions and when to remain silent. She wanted desperately to talk about this situation with him, but it was Peggy's secret and not Lexi's to tell. Egg and Binky were still carrying on when they arrived at the health club.

"You think you're so smart! I'll bet you don't even know *how* to play racquetball!" Binky accused sourly as Egg tried to list the fundamentals of the game for his sister.

Egg's face got red and splotchy. Lexi was expecting to see steam coming out his ears any moment when Todd stepped in to calm things down.

"Why don't Binky and I use the court for awhile first, Egg? I can show her a few shots and get her acquainted with the feel of the racquet before we try playing a game. You and Lexi can use the treadmill or lift weights to warm up. How about that?"

"Fine with me," Egg blustered. "I'm not sure why I even thought I could teach Binky this game. She never believes anything I say."

"If you wouldn't tease her so much, she'd probably trust you more," Todd pointed out cheerfully.

Egg gave a wicked grin. "Oh, yeah."

Lexi looped her hand around Egg's scrawny elbow. "Come on. First one to the weight room gets her choice of machines."

"You mean *his* choice," Egg retorted and plunged ahead.

Lexi had put three kilometers on the ski machine when Todd came loping down the stairs. "Your turn Eggo, my man. Your sister wants to take you on."

"You're kidding, right?" Egg said in disbelief. Still, he swung off the slantboard and headed for the courts. "She wants to be creamed by me. The girl is a glutton for punishment."

As Egg disappeared, Lexi asked, "How was Binky's first lesson?"

Todd chuckled. "The girl is a natural. She'll run circles around Egg in no time. She wants to show off."

They were both laughing when Jerry Randall came storming into the weight room. His eyes were cloudy and his expression black. Without saying hello, he moved toward the weights. Silently, he began to do arm curls until his face was red and his cheeks were puffed out like those of a gopher.

When he stopped to rest, Todd inquired calmly, "Bad day, Jerry?"

"None of your business."

"I don't know about that. Lexi and I were here first."

Jerry scowled. "I need to blow off some steam. Do you mind?"

Todd shrugged. "I thought your parents were here. Why aren't you home with them?"

Jerry's scowl deepened. "I couldn't take any more."

Lexi felt a nudge of surprise. "But you were so anxious for them to come!"

"Yeah, but the feeling wasn't mutual."

Lexi and Todd exchanged a puzzled glance. Todd's next question was cautious. "You mean they didn't want to be here?"

"Not any longer than necessary. They're just 'checking in' to see if I'm behaving." Jerry's bullish bravado seemed to dissolve before their eyes. He lay on the weight bench, his body slack. The angry mask was replaced by a look of miserable frustration. "I thought they'd stay this time."

"What about their jobs?"

Jerry swung his feet to the floor and returned Todd's steady gaze. "What about *me*? Far as I can tell, they'd be happier if I'd never been born!"

"Jerry, I—"

"They came home to see if I'd gotten into any more trouble. They wanted to make sure I wasn't giving my aunt and uncle too many headaches, that's all." Jerry's tone was hurt and bitter. "Maybe I *should* give them a few problems if that's what they're looking for."

Todd moved quietly toward Jerry. "I think you'd better tell them how you feel. Maybe they don't realize how hard it is on you to live without them."

"What makes you think they'd listen?"

"They came to check on you. The least you can do is tell them what's going on." Todd was thoughtful for a moment, then added, "It's better to tell them than to jump angrily behind the wheel of a car and have another accident."

At that, Jerry spun around on the toe of his tennis shoe and left the room.

Todd gave a low whistle beneath his breath as they watched him leave. "There goes one guy who really needs his parents." Lexi nodded. She knew of another person who needed her parents just as much. The rest of the afternoon Lexi could concentrate on nothing but Peggy.

———

It was late Sunday evening when the telephone rang. Intuitively, Lexi knew who was calling.

"Lexi? Can we talk?"

"My parents are in the other room if that's what you mean."

"Mine just went out for a drive. They asked me if I wanted to come and I told them I had homework."

"Do you?"

"Of course! What do you think I'd do, lie to . . ." Peggy's voice faded.

"Have you told them about the baby?"

"Don't call it a baby, Lexi. It's a fetus—"

"Then you haven't told them."

"I just couldn't—"

"Then that's as good as lying to them, Peg! Don't you see?"

There was a long silence on the other end of the line. When Peggy began to speak, her voice was quavery.

"Listen, could you come over for awhile? I really need to talk to somebody."

Lexi glanced at her watch. "For a little while. Hang on. I'll be right there."

The only light on in the Madison household was a small reading lamp in the living room. Peggy was curled on the window seat on the far side of the room, bathed in shadows. Having let herself in, Lexi walked silently across the floor to sit by her friend.

"I talked to Rita about her abortion," Peggy blurted.

"Did you tell her you were—"

"Are you kidding? I just made sure the subject came up in a roundabout way and then started asking questions. I don't think she suspected anything. She's talked to others about it."

Lexi had a sick feeling in the pit of her stomach. She couldn't quit thinking about that paraphrase she'd written of Psalm 139. *You made me, God, intestines and all. You put me together, like a jigsaw puzzle, right there in my mother's womb.*

"What did she say?"

Peggy looked a little green even in the dim light. "She said it was scary, but it was over pretty fast. She had a D & C."

Lexi looked blank.

"She said that meant dilation and curettage. It's scraping the inside of your womb so that there's . . . nothing . . . there anymore." Peggy's voice lowered. "I guess there are other ways too. Rita called it a suction abortion. Sort of like vacuuming out your insides, I guess."

"Peggy," Lexi began, but Peggy wouldn't let her continue.

Voice artificially bright, Peggy kept talking. "Rita says sometimes girls wait too long and then it's harder to do. The doctor can make you go into labor and deliver the baby or else you can have surgery. I wouldn't want to wait that long. It would be easier if—"

"Are you listening to yourself?" Lexi blurted. "There's *nothing* easy about what you're talking about! You can't make decisions like this without talking to your parents! And didn't you listen to *anything* I said about what's in the Psalms? Have you thought about what it is God might want you to do?"

"But what about what *I* want to do?" Peggy's face was contorted with distress. "What else *can* I do? I'm too young to have a baby! It would ruin everything for me! It's already ruining things between me and Chad." Peggy clamped a hand over her lips as if that bit of information was not meant to come out.

"You and Chad are having trouble?"

Peggy's shoulders slumped even farther. "He's edgy, that's all. I think he's mad because I let this happen."

Lexi gave a snort. "And where was he? Doesn't he think he has any responsibility for this?"

"He says we can get married, but we're not even done with high school yet! Chad wants to go to college." Her voice broke and she whispered, "I did too."

Lexi remained silent as Peggy rose and began to pace around the darkened room. She was talking more to herself than to Lexi.

"Coach told me on Friday that I could be a starter for the team for sure. I'm the youngest one on varsity. It's a real honor and now . . ." She rubbed ruefully at her stomach. "I wish I didn't feel so sick all the time. I'm afraid someone will find out and I'll be kicked off the team without ever getting a chance to show anyone how good I could be."

Peggy drifted to the couch and sat down. "Nobody's ever going to know what I'm good at—maybe not even me. How am I supposed to make plans for college now? Maybe all I'm good at is making a mess of things." Her eyes flooded with tears. "I've really done that, Lexi."

A harsh, unlovely laugh escaped her. "My family is still talking about going to London so my dad can do research. I think it would be the most wonderful place in the world to visit. But now . . ." Peggy slammed her fist into the cushiony soft pillows on the davenport. "This baby has ruined my life!"

"I'm not sure it's the baby you should be angry with, Peggy," Lexi said softly.

Peggy's face crumpled. "I know. It didn't ask to exist. But I didn't ask it to exist either!"

"In a way you did," Lexi pointed out. "You and Chad made some choices."

"Great choices," Peggy said bitterly. "What we were doing seemed okay at the time. It was romantic, I guess. I never thought about what might happen until *after* we'd . . ." Her voice faded. "And then it was too late and I'd put it out of my mind until the next time . . ."

"Talk to your parents, Peggy. Please?" Lexi pleaded. "I can't help you with this. I've been praying and reading the Bible, but you don't seem to want to listen to me." Lexi gave a weak smile. "Actually, I don't blame you. I've probably been pretty hard on you."

Peggy smiled weakly. "It's okay. I know how strong your faith is, Lexi, and I did listen to what you said even though it might not have seemed that way. It's just that I'm not old enough or smart enough to have this baby, Lexi. I'm too young! What else can I do?"

Chapter Nine

The Emerald Tones were rehearsing in the music room, but Lexi could not seem to keep her mind on the music. Her head was too full of Peggy's troubles.

She managed to muddle through the rehearsal without making obvious mistakes that would have drawn Mrs. Waverly's attention to her. But she was thankful when the music teacher wrapped things up and dismissed the group for the afternoon.

Todd sauntered over to her from the men's section as the group disbanded. "You're looking mighty grim today," he commented. "Something on your mind?"

Lexi shrugged. "Oh, nothing in particular, just some . . . questions."

Todd nodded as if he comprehended her vague statement fully. "Want to talk about it?" he asked. "My car is in my brother's garage today, so I'm on foot. Maybe we could walk to the Hamburger Shack." He paused before adding, "Sometimes you think better in fresh air."

Lexi nodded. She always felt calm in Todd's presence. Perhaps he could give her some direction, even though she knew she couldn't reveal to him what was worrying her.

They gathered their jackets from their lockers and left the school. They walked side by side down the sidewalk, hands jammed snugly into their pockets, shoulders rolled forward slightly and each taking long, shuffling steps. Todd did not press her for a long while. Lexi remained silent.

"Todd," she finally began. "What would you do if . . ." She paused again. It was hard to formulate the words in just the right way. She didn't want Todd suspecting anything until Peggy was ready to reveal her condition. "What would you do if one of your friends was in a lot of trouble and wouldn't talk to his parents about it?"

Todd gave Lexi a sharp glance. "A lot of trouble? What kind of trouble?"

Lexi's eyes were vague and unfocused. "Oh, just any kind of trouble. Serious trouble."

"Like with the police?" he asked.

"Maybe not that serious." Then she paused. "Well, maybe it is. But a different kind of trouble. More personal trouble."

"Like when Jennifer was diagnosed as dyslexic?" he pressed. "That kind of trouble? When she was rebelling and making a fool of herself?"

"Kind of, only more serious than that. Trouble that . . . affects more people."

Todd's forehead furrowed in a confused frown. "I'm not quite sure what you mean, Lexi."

Lexi waved her hand in the air. "Never mind. It doesn't matter what kind of trouble your friend is in.

It just matters that he won't tell his parents that he's in trouble and they're the only ones who could help him."

"Well, if he wouldn't talk to his parents, maybe he'd talk to someone else. Mrs. Waverly or the coach or the school counselor, somebody like that. Would that help?"

"Maybe," Lexi agreed, doubtfully. "If this person would talk to someone like that. But, if she, I mean he, wouldn't tell his parents, why would he go to someone who is even more of a stranger at the school?"

"Well, sometimes it's easier to talk to strangers or people we don't know very well," Todd commented. "We're not so worried about disappointing them." He grinned impishly. "One of the things that keeps me on the straight and narrow is the fact that it would break my parents' hearts if I didn't live up to their expectations in some way. Of course, it doesn't hurt knowing that my brother Mike would break my head too!"

Lexi gave a weak smile, but she persisted. "If you were the only person who knew anything about your friend's secret and about the problem and she, I mean he, wouldn't tell anyone else, wouldn't you feel responsible?"

Todd nodded, his eyes wide. "That's a pretty heavy load to carry, that's for sure. Does this friend expect you to do something to help in some way?"

"I don't know," Lexi sighed. "There are some things that only adults can handle, not other kids."

Todd nodded sagely. "That's true. But if this friend won't go to anyone for help, I'm not sure there would be anything you or I could do." He looked at her with a wise expression on his features. "Sometimes friends just have to be there for one another."

"That just doesn't seem like enough," Lexi protested.

Todd's step slowed to a halt and he turned to look Lexi directly in the eye. "I don't know who you're talking about, Lexi, or what kind of trouble this person is in, but it sounds to me like it's too big for you to handle alone."

Lexi's shoulders drooped defeatedly. Todd was right. What Peggy needed now was the support of her family, her minister and the advice of a doctor, not advice from other teenagers.

She and Todd walked quietly for a long time. Finally, Todd broke the silence with a comment. "I think Jerry and his parents are having a pretty bad time right now."

Lexi nodded. "He's disappointed, isn't he? He thought that this time they'd move back and he could live with them again."

"Can you blame him?"

They were both considering Jerry's troubles when they heard Egg McNaughton yelling behind them. "Hey! Wait up. Wait up, you guys. Wait for me."

They turned around to see Egg running like a disjointed scarecrow down the sidewalk. He was waving one arm and clutching a stack of school books with the other. Egg was on a growing spurt this year and he looked like a stickman made of scrawny arms and legs. He was huffing and puffing as he caught up to them.

"Do you mind if I join you? You're going to the Hamburger Shack, aren't you?"

Todd nodded. "Sure. What's up?"

A gloomy cloud seemed to settle over Egg's features. "Nothing good, that's for sure."

"Oh?" Lexi asked suspiciously. "What do you mean by that?"

"I just came from the newsroom." Egg rolled his eyes. "Something's going on and I can't find out what it is."

"Going on? What do you mean?"

"With Minda."

Lexi got a sinking sensation in the pit of her stomach. "Minda's up to something?"

Egg nodded. "Minda's always up to something. This time I think it's something bad."

"Why do you say that?" Todd asked, frowning. "What's she done now?"

Minda was a master troublemaker around the school and everyone knew that when she went into action, no good was going to come of it.

"She and a bunch of her club members, the Hi-Fives, were hanging out in the press room, giggling in a tight little huddle. Every time I got too near, they clammed up like they didn't want me to hear what they were discussing."

"Sounds bad," Todd said with a nod.

"Minda asked me if she could lay out her own column this month," Egg went on to say.

"That's pretty strange too, knowing Minda," Todd said. "Normally, she doesn't do any extra work unless someone forces her into it."

Egg nodded morosely. "She's usually the first one

to hand her column over. This month, I haven't seen it at all. She wants to set it up herself on the computer and get it all laid out."

"What do you think she's writing?" Lexi wondered.

"Well, if it's her fashion column, she's invented some new and revolutionary sort of accessory to knock every guy's eyes out," Todd said with a laugh. "Or, if it's the gossip column, then the entire Cedar River High School better look out, because nobody's safe."

"I'm afraid it's the gossip column this time," Egg groaned. "I tried to talk her into letting me lay it out, but Mrs. Drummond is taking a few days off to try to get over her bursitis. The lady who's subbing for her thinks everything's okay. Said it was fine with her if Minda wanted to lay out her own column."

"Mrs. Drummond must not have been feeling well if she forgot to warn her about Minda," Todd said with a chuckle.

"Trouble. I'm sure it's trouble," Egg went on gloomily, his long face hanging even longer.

By then, they'd reached the Hamburger Shack. All three of them stood outside and looked up at the flashing neon sign. Then they exchanged glances. "Are you hungry?"

"Not anymore."

"Me either. In fact, my stomach kinda hurts."

"Maybe we should just go home, Todd," Lexi suggested, "now that we've gotten ourselves all worked up."

"Yeah," Egg agreed. "I hate to waste my money on a burger when I'm feeling like this."

Todd nodded. "All right. I'll walk you home, Lexi. We'll see you later, Eggo, my man."

Egg half lifted a hand in a discouraged wave and meandered off in the direction of his house. Lexi and Todd turned onto the street that led past the Leighton home.

"Looks like everybody's home," Lexi announced. The lights were on in every single window and she could hear music thrumming from the house.

"Maybe this is where the action's at," Todd said, glancing around. "I see your mom and Ben jumping around inside."

Lexi led the way to the front door and into the foyer. "Don't touch anything," her mother yelled from the living room. "Take you coat off and hang it in the hallway and step very carefully. Most of these paintings are wet."

Lexi and Todd moved into the living room, which was a bright collage of color from end to end. There were daisies and roses and irises splashed onto large, white canvases. There were landscapes and florals wherever they looked. In one corner was a large portrait of Ben and Lexi when they were much younger and another recent portrait of Mr. Leighton himself.

"What's going on, Mom?"

Mrs. Leighton propped her hands on the narrow shelf of her hips and looked around the room. "I just got a call today. I have a chance to do a showing in a local gallery. The show that they were planning to exhibit was cancelled for some reason and they were scrambling to find something to put in its place. They got ahold of my name and they called me. Of course, I agreed. Then I realized that I was several pictures short, so I did some quick florals and I dug things out of the attic. Well, what do you think? Will it make up a show?"

Todd glanced around the room in admiration. "This is great. I didn't know you were so talented, Mrs. Leighton."

Lexi's mom gave him a nervous smile. "Thank you, Todd. That's exactly what I needed to hear. This is very nerve-racking, you know. I am only an amateur."

"You're an almost professional, Mom," Lexi defended. "Don't put yourself down. Look how many paintings you've done in the past few weeks."

Mrs. Leighton nodded. "Too many, I'm afraid, when I see them all displayed here in the living room. Do you think that maybe I've gone a little bit overboard in reaction to my boredom?"

"Boredom?" Todd echoed. "How could you be bored?"

Mrs. Leighton ran her fingers through her dark hair. "You didn't hear about my little episode, Todd? About how depressed I was feeling now that Lexi and Ben don't seem to need me anymore?"

"We do need you, Mom," Lexi protested, but her mother just waved her hand in the air and continued.

"Ben's doing so beautifully at the Academy and he's getting to be so independent that I feel as if I'm not needed nearly so much by him anymore. And Lexi, well, you know how independent she is, Todd."

Todd grinned at Lexi. "I sure do. That's one of my favorite things about her."

Lexi socked Todd in the arm with a fist. "It drives you crazy and you know it."

Todd laughed again. "I'll never tell."

Mrs. Leighton was still standing in the middle of the living room surveying her creations. "You know? All the painting I've been doing has been great fun, but still, my favorite thing is being home and being a mom." She gave Lexi a fond look. "You kids provided me with some of the best years of my life, Lexi, whether you realize it or not."

"Some of the best and some of the worst, I'll bet," Todd muttered under his breath.

Lexi balled up her fist to give him another punch, but he ducked out of the way.

"I think I'd better be going now. It looks pretty busy around here. Your paintings are great, Mrs. Leighton. See you later." With a wink toward Lexi, Todd ducked out the front door. She could hear his voice trail back to her as he moved down the sidewalk. "Good night. See you tomorrow."

Inside, Lexi moved toward her mother and curled her arms around her waist. "You know, Mom, we still need you, no matter what you think. I can't understand it. Where would this family be without you?"

Mrs. Leighton threw an arm around Lexi's shoulder. "I'm glad to hear you say that, honey. But you and Ben have gotten very independent. I'm thankful that I have my painting to fall back on when I'm bored out of my mind. Now, if only your father would get home to help me put some of these things in cartons and load them into the car. . . . I have to go over to the art gallery tonight and help hang the show."

Mrs. Leighton snapped her fingers. "Oh, I almost forgot. I had a roast I was going to put in for supper." She glanced at her watch. "Well, it's too late now. Do you want to fry some eggs, Lexi, and make a little toast? Would that be all right for supper? Or maybe there's a frozen pizza in the freezer somewhere, if you just dig long enough. Don't mind the paint palate that's lying on top. I wanted to keep my paints to do some touch-ups so I stuck them in the freezer. They're covered with wax paper. Don't smear them on anything."

Mrs. Leighton was still distractedly giving directions when Lexi went into the kitchen. There were dishes in the sink and Lexi noted a trace of green mold on the loaf of bread in the cupboard.

She shook her head. She was glad that her mom was having such a wonderful time, but she did miss at least a little bit of the old mom who thought she was needed enough to remember the roast at suppertime.

Lexi set the table and scrambled a batch of eggs with mushrooms and grated cheese.

The family had just finished their meal when the doorbell rang.

"I'll get it, Mom," Lexi offered and jumped up from her place.

"Then I guess that leaves Ben and I to do the dishes," Mr. Leighton observed.

Lexi moved toward the front door. She could see Egg and Binky standing on the other side of the leaded glass, peering in at her.

"Hello! What are you two doing here?" she asked with surprise. "Didn't I just see you Egg?"

"Binky wanted to come over and talk to you," Egg explained, giving his sister a dirty look. "And she made me come along."

"Well, that was nice of you," Lexi said, smiling at Egg. "Now she won't have to walk home alone in the dark."

"Oh, be quiet," Binky told her brother. "You're upset too and you know it. You just aren't letting on, that's all."

"Upset?" Lexi looked from Egg to Binky and back again. "What are you upset about?"

"I stayed after school today to practice my clarinet," Binky explained as she moved into the house. Lexi indicated with her hand that they should go into her father's den instead of the living room, which was still cluttered with paintings.

"After I was done and I put my instrument away, I went back to my locker to get my books. I could still hear the girls in the gym practicing for the basketball game, so I decided to just peek in and see how they were doing."

"And?" Lexi asked. "How were they doing?"

Binky shuddered. "I wish I'd never looked. They were scrimmaging and while I was watching, Peggy Madison made some big blunder that upset the coach—"

"Oh-oh," Lexi muttered under her breath.

Binky continued. "The coach really gave her a talking to and instead of just listening and nodding, Peggy started talking back. The whole thing escalated all out of proportion and Peggy was screaming and crying at the coach. The coach was ordering her off the floor and . . . It was awful, Lexi! The coach's face was all red and angry, and Peggy just got whiter and whiter until I thought she was going to faint. She stormed off the floor, but I noticed that when she got to the locker-room door, she had to hang on to the doorjamb to steady herself. It was as if she got dizzy from all that yelling."

Lexi closed her eyes. *Oh, Peggy. Not this too,* she thought to herself. She opened her eyes and looked at Egg. "Is that what you're upset about too, Egg?"

Egg looked gloomy. "Binky's got a big mouth." He turned to his sister. "You didn't have to tell her anything about what I think, Binky. It was no big deal; he was just in a bad mood, that's all."

Binky turned to Lexi. "Chad Allen wouldn't speak to Egg tonight. They ran into each other on Egg's way home from the Hamburger Shack and Egg said Chad acted really weird."

"I didn't say weird, exactly," Egg protested. "I just said he acted a little funny."

"A little funny? Weird? What's the difference?" Binky asked. "He wouldn't even speak to Egg. He wouldn't even say hello. And then, when Egg tried to talk about school, Chad just cut him off. He said he didn't have time to worry about schoolwork. He said if that was Egg's biggest problem, then he was pretty lucky. I think he was rude," Binky announced.

Binky was trembling like a little wet hen and her face was furious. It was all right for Binky to run Egg down, Lexi observed, but it was completely unacceptable for anyone outside the family to say a harsh word to her brother.

"Everyone has bad days," Lexi pointed out, hoping that neither of the pair noticed the nervous quiver in her voice. "Maybe Chad did have a lot on his mind. Who knows? He could have flunked a test or something today."

"Maybe," Egg said doubtfully. "I don't know, but he was acting really strange."

"Speaking of strange," Binky piped up. "Did Egg tell you about Minda and her column?"

Lexi nodded. "He thinks that Minda's gonna try and stir up some trouble."

"I don't think so, I *know* so," Egg said unhappily. "And Mrs. Drummond's gonna be mad if she does, because she'll have expected me to stop it. But if her substitute says it's okay, how can I stop Minda?"

"It's not your fault, Egg," Lexi soothed. "Mrs. Drummond understands about Minda."

Egg snorted, "Well, then she's the only one who does."

"What's this?" Lexi said. "Egg McNaughton saying something negative about the wonderful Minda Hannaford? Why, Egg, is your infatuation with Minda starting to fade?"

Egg blushed to a deep carrot red. "I like Minda. I like her a lot. But that doesn't mean I don't understand how she can be." He rolled his eyes. "More than anyone, I should understand how Minda can be."

Binky had sunk gloomily to the couch. She was perched on the edge like a tiny sparrow might perch on a telephone wire; her scrawny elbows were on her knees and her hands cupped her pointed chin.

"Something's going on," she announced to no one in particular. "First Peggy, then Chad, now Minda. They're all going crazy. What's wrong with everyone?"

Chapter Ten

"Dad, can I have a ride to school today? Otherwise I'm going to be really late." Lexi tugged a brush through her hair with one hand and tried to pry her foot into a tennis shoe with the other. The clock was creeping toward eight-thirty.

"I can't believe we all overslept!" Mr. Leighton jerked at his necktie and grimaced into the mirror. "I haven't done that in years. Usually Ben is up with the birds. His singing wakes me up before the alarm clock."

"He stayed up too late at the gallery opening," Mrs. Leighton groaned. Her hair was rumpled and she was still in her nightgown. "I knew we should have gotten a sitter for Ben."

"But he loved seeing your work on display," Mr. Leighton pointed out. "We all did."

Lexi nodded in agreement. It had been a very exciting evening, seeing her mother's art work hung and lit so carefully that every piece looked as though it had been painted by some famous artist. There'd been a harpist playing and the gallery served tea, coffee and tiny cookies to the patrons who came. Mrs. Leighton, in a long black skirt and white silk blouse, had greeted them and answered questions about her work. Lexi had been very impressed.

"Good. But now we're all paying the price," Mrs. Leighton remarked. "I'll drive Ben to the Academy if you'll drop Lexi off at school."

Lexi sat impatiently in the car waiting for her father. She hated to be late for school because it took her several minutes to open the combination on her locker and exchange her books for the ones she needed for morning classes.

Just then Mr. Leighton burst through the door and jumped into the car. He managed to get her to the school in record time and the last bell had not yet rung when Lexi gathered her books and rushed into class.

As she hurried into the room, Lexi noticed an odd aura of silence. Were they all staring at her? she wondered. She was rarely this late in getting to class. Then, as she glanced around, she noticed that everyone was deeply involved in reading the latest copy of the *River Review*.

She'd almost forgotten that this was the day it came out. There was usually some curiosity about what the school paper held, but today everyone seemed abnormally interested in the news.

Before Lexi could borrow a copy and see what the hot new item of interest was, the bell rang and class began. Quickly she forgot about the newspaper and what it might contain.

"What's going on today, anyway?" Lexi wondered to Binky as they made their way to the lunchroom at noon. "Everybody is acting really strange. Did I miss something by getting here so late?"

Binky gave Lexi a sideways glance. "You mean you don't know?"

"Know what?"

"About Minda Hannaford's column?"

Lexi gave her friend a wary look. "What about Minda's column?"

Binky reached over to the stack of "Reviews" sitting near the lunchroom door. "Here. Read it for yourself. There's no way I can explain it to you."

Lexi thumbed through the pages to find the column. Minda's smile beamed out at her from beneath a cloud of blond curls. Lexi scanned the page and her eyes widened.

Binky nodded. "It's a nasty one, that's for sure. Minda must have been taking ugly pills for days to work herself up for this one."

Lexi stared at the column.

> Who's the boy who can't seem to keep his parents at home? Are you sure it's not something you said—or did?

"Jerry?" Lexi whispered.

"That's my guess. Minda knows how sensitive Jerry is about his parents being gone so much. And she probably realized before he did that this last visit wasn't going to be any different than the ones before. They've always gone back to their work whether it's in Alaska or the Persian Gulf."

"That's mean."

Binky shrugged. "You haven't even gotten to the mean part yet."

Lexi again dropped her eyes to the written page. There were dozens of cruel little barbs written in Minda's breezy, carefree style. Lexi could just imagine her shaking her blond head and shooting off one slam after another, not caring how the people she was referring to were affected.

Then her gaze fell on a sentence that nearly leapt off the page.

> And who *is* the girl last seen buying *very suspicious* items in the mall drugstore? Any special reason that she's so interested in the dirty gossip about what's happened to others in her situation? Will we be hearing wedding bells?

Lexi felt her mouth drop open, but she didn't have the will to shut it. She was absolutely dumbfounded. *It was Peggy that Minda was referring to!*

Rita must have told Minda that Peggy was asking about her abortion. Minda had added that together with the day she'd seen Lexi and Peggy coming from the drugstore mall and put two and two together. No doubt Minda had only been guessing, but she'd come up with the right answer!

Binky peered over Lexi's shoulder. "I don't know who Minda was talking about, but it's pretty rotten. She's making it sound like whoever she's writing about is"—Binky shrugged her thin shoulders—". . . I don't know. Pregnant or something."

Lexi crumpled the paper into a ball and threw it into the trash. "It's a rotten column and a dirty trick, that's all I can say."

Binky looked at her in surprise. "Yeah. I think so

too. But I didn't think you'd get all upset about it. Minda's always doing crummy things. You know that."

"But think about the girl in the column! We recognized Jerry even though Minda didn't use his name. What about the poor girl?"

"I never thought about it that way," Binky admitted. "That would be terrible!"

"And I doubt that Minda ever puts her brain in gear at all!"

Binky stared at Lexi. "I don't think I've ever seen you so upset!"

Lexi forced herself to control her voice. "It's just that I'm tired of Minda being so mean. Maybe the girl in the column doesn't even exist, but that's no reason to . . ." Lexi's voice trailed away. She couldn't even talk about this right now. She had to see Peggy. What must she be going through?

It wasn't until after school that Lexi had the opportunity to talk to Peggy.

They were alone in the girls' bathroom. Lexi turned on a faucet full blast. "So no one will hear us talk," she whispered. Peggy nodded and turned on another faucet.

When she turned to Lexi, her face was contorted with fear.

"What am I going to do, Lexi? Now that Minda has put that in the paper, somebody's going to guess it's me she's talking about!"

"Calm down, Peg. That isn't necessarily so!"

"Sure it is. Rita guessed what I wanted the abortion information for and she told Minda! Now probably every Hi-Five knows. How long do you think they'll keep a secret?"

Peggy was right, of course. Lexi stared at the floor.

"And my parents always read the 'Review'! They know what day it comes out and my mom asks for it as soon as I walk in the door! They say it's a good way for them to keep up on what's happening at school." Peggy slumped against the wall. "Too good."

"You've got to tell them before they figure something out for themselves. You've got to tell them anyway, but now there's no time to lose. This is too big a problem for kids to handle alone, Peggy. I want to help you but I can't. *You've got to tell them.*"

Peggy stared at the ugly green tile on the wall, her eyes fixed and glassy. "I'm not sure my mom and dad will agree to an abortion," she said softly. Lexi noticed that she was rubbing her stomach gently. "They're pretty hung up on that sort of thing."

"There are other options, Peg. I'm sure there are," Lexi pleaded. "Don't rush in to anything without—"

Peggy suddenly turned to leave the bathroom. "I'll tell them."

"Call me when you're done?"

"If they'll let me." Peggy gave a soft groan. "I don't deserve to be trusted to do anything right anymore. They'll never forgive me, Lexi. And they probably never should. I've done something that I can't be forgiven for." Without another word, she left the room.

Lexi turned off the faucets and waited a minute before following.

————

Binky and Lexi walked home together; Lexi was glad for Binky's nonstop chatter that needed no responses. Binky didn't even realize that Lexi had said no more than five words all the time they were together. Lexi waved a goodbye to her friend and hurried inside.

To avoid being questioned by Ben or her mother, Lexi mounted the stairs two at a time to her room. Her Bible was lying on the nightstand by her bed and she picked it up.

Opening the Book, she turned to Romans. As her eyes skimmed the pages, verse upon verse seemed to leap out at her.

"All men . . . are under the power of sin. . . . None is righteous, no, not one" (Rom. 3:9–10).

"All have sinned and fallen short of the glory of God" (Rom. 3:23).

Lexi's heart began to beat a little faster and her gaze skimmed the pages.

"But God shows his love for us in that while we were yet sinners Christ died for us" (Rom. 5:8).

It was all here! Everything that Peggy needed to hear was written on these pages!

"We rejoice in God through our Lord Jesus Christ, through whom we have now received our reconciliation" (Rom. 5:12).

And, "There is therefore now no condemnation for those who are in Christ Jesus. For the law of the Spirit of life in Christ Jesus has set me free from the law of sin and death" (Rom. 8:1).

Lexi lifted her head, her eyes shining. Romans

said it better than she ever could.

This book was over nineteen hundred years old, Lexi marveled, and it told of people suffering from the same types of doubts and worries that Peggy had at this very moment.

Everyone is a sinner. There isn't one single person who isn't. They've all fallen short of God's glory. Peggy knew she'd fallen short. After all, at some time or other, everyone has. But even though we're all so weak and sinful, God loved us enough to send His Son, Jesus, to die on the cross. Because of that, everyone who believes in Christ is free! Free from the sins they've committed and free to live a new life!

If God can forgive Peggy, then surely her parents will. And if her parents can help her, then God will surely be doing that too. Maybe there is some hope in all of this, Lexi mused. *With God working for Peggy— and her parents doing everything they can to help, then surely whatever Peggy decides and whatever happens to her next will be all right.*

The ring of the telephone broke into Lexi's thoughts.

"Lexi! Tel'fone!" Ben yelled from downstairs.

Lexi reached for the upstairs extension. Maybe it was Peggy.

"How are you?" Todd's voice was soft and pleasant.

"Fine. How are you?" Lexi tried to keep the disappointment from her voice.

"Not so great."

"What's wrong?" Todd never admitted that things were wrong!

"It's Jerry. He's pretty upset by Minda's column."

"Oh, that." Lexi had almost forgotten about that part of the column. "Tell him not to worry. Everybody knows what Minda is like." Lexi hoped her words were true.

"I have been. I think I've got him calmed down for the time being, but if anyone asks him about it tomorrow I'm afraid he might explode."

"Would it help if I called him?"

"The only thing that would help is a retraction," Todd said acidly. Then he became quiet. "Say, that's an idea ... Gotta go, Lexi. I've got some calls to make."

Before Lexi could say another word, Todd had hung up.

———

Mealtime was over and the evening stretched long before Lexi. She still hadn't heard from Peggy. She and Ben put together a jigsaw puzzle and she finished her homework.

The hand of the clock was edging toward ten when the telephone rang again. Lexi reached eagerly for the receiver.

"Hello?"

"Lexi? It's Peggy."

Lexi gave a sigh of relief. "I've been waiting and waiting for you to call."

"Well, we told them."

"We?"

"Chad came over. He said I shouldn't have to do it alone."

Give Chad a point for bravery, Lexi thought to herself. At least he was taking that much responsibility for his part in Peggy's pregnancy.

"He told them that we wanted to get married."

Lexi drew a breath of surprise. "And?"

"They said we were too young."

"Were they angry?"

"Not as bad as I thought. Mom cried and Dad . . . he just paced the floor and kept saying 'My little girl, my little girl' until I thought I'd scream. They were really good, Lexi. You were right. I should have told them sooner."

"So what are you going to do?" Lexi was afraid to mouth the word abortion for fear that's what they'd decided.

"My dad asked me about an abortion. He and Chad thought maybe that's what I should do. I was surprised," Peggy admitted. "Dad must have been pretty shook up to suggest it."

"And what do you think?"

The line was silent for a long time.

"It's what I wanted to do. At first, at least. Get rid of it. Pretend it didn't happen. Pretend Chad and I weren't foolish enough to have had sex and made a baby." Peggy sighed. "But then I began to think about what you said."

"Me?" Lexi squeaked. "What was that?"

"About God knowing about a baby before even the parents do. About Him forming a baby inside its mother. And about Him knowing how long a baby will live even before it's lived at all." Peggy's voice quivered. "Deep down, I think He means for this baby to live longer than just a few months, Lexi. I think He's got better plans than that for this one."

Her voice began to tremble. "I just can't do it. I can't have an abortion."

Lexi silently thanked God for this answer to her prayer.

Peggy continued. "Maybe Rita could have an abortion. I thought I could do it too, but I realize now that I was wrong." Peggy laughed a soft, humorless laugh. "I can't do that to a life that I was responsible for starting. Chad and I made the mistake, not this baby. Now we have to try to make things as right as we can."

Then Peggy said something very odd. "Were you praying for me tonight, Lexi?"

Lexi thought back to the time she'd spent in her room, to the book of Romans. "Yes, I was."

"I *knew* it!" Peggy's voice was triumphant. "I *could* feel it. It was as if something inside told me that yes, I had sinned, but that there's still hope for me. I think I finally know what it means to 'repent' like we always hear about in church. Lexi, I'm honestly sorry for what Chad and I did. When I pray tonight that's just what I'm going to tell Jesus. I want to live a new, clean life."

Lexi swallowed the lump in her throat. She'd grown up hearing about the power of prayer. She'd even experienced it sometimes, but never so directly, so intensely.

"You sound very . . . grown up, Peggy," Lexi observed shakily.

"I feel like I've aged about fifty years in the last five weeks," she admitted. "But I guess I needed to grow up. You're the only person I could say this to, Lexi, and be sure they'd understand. But I just figured out tonight that the decisions I make now have eternal significance."

Eternal significance.

Big words. Not like those Peggy usually used. But it was true. What Peggy did next was going to matter a great deal to the new little life within her.

Chapter Eleven

Todd caught up with Lexi as she left the school. She felt his strong hand wrap gently around her elbow and she looked up into his somber blue eyes.

"In a hurry?"

"Not really," she admitted. "Ben has a dentist appointment after school, so I have to get home to put supper in the oven. Nothing else."

"Do you mind if I walk you home?"

"Of course not."

Todd was behaving very strangely, Lexi thought. He seemed so . . . intense. They were silent as they walked the blocks to Lexi's house.

"Want to come in?" she asked as they stood at the front door. "Mom made chocolate chip cookies last night. I think Ben managed to leave a couple alone."

He smiled weakly. "Sure. Why not?"

Seated across the table from each other, a plate of cookies and a quart of milk between them, Todd finally told her what was on his mind.

"I talked to Chad last night."

Lexi looked down at the napkin in front of her

rather than to stare him squarely in the eye. "Oh?"

"You don't have to worry about letting their secret slip. Chad told me about Peggy and the baby."

Lexi looked up. "I suppose they're both worried about Minda's column."

Todd shrugged. "That's the least of their problems, if you ask me." He chewed thoughtfully on his lower lip for a long moment. "Chad's a pretty cool guy but this really has him panicked."

"No wonder."

"He's scared, Lexi. Scared that if Peggy decides to keep the baby, it's going to ruin all the plans he's made for the future." Todd averted his eyes. "And he's scared that if she *doesn't* keep it, neither one of them will ever get over the guilt."

At least Chad's thought about it that much, Lexi noted to herself. Sometimes it seemed as if Peggy were in this all by herself.

"He told me that he offered to marry Peggy but her parents said no."

"They said they were too young."

Todd's head nodded furiously. "That's for sure. I wonder what he was thinking about when it happened . . ." Then he blushed. "Never mind, I know what he was thinking about. It just wasn't the future."

He drummed his fingers on the tabletop. "Chad should have known better. My mom has had some pretty frank talks with me about . . . you know."

"But not everyone has parents who can talk to their teenagers about things like sex before marriage," Lexi said frankly. "And not everyone has a church or Sunday school class that is willing to face those kinds of issues. We've had some good guidance, Todd."

He nodded. "I suppose. But I still think it's stupid to let yourself get into the kind of predicament they're in. There's no way out for them, Lexi. None at all."

No way out.

"That sounds pretty final, Todd."

"It does. But it's true."

Lexi frowned, confused by what Todd meant.

"I just think that no matter what happens next, somebody pays a price. There's no way to get through this situation without some kind of pain."

She nodded. What he was saying made sense. "You mean that either Chad and Peggy get into an early marriage that neither really wants . . ."

" . . . Or they give up the baby and spend the rest of their lives wondering who he is and what he looks like and if his adoptive parents are treating him right . . ."

" . . . Or Peggy has an abortion and they have to handle the guilt and the memory for the rest of their lives."

"And there's the baby to think about."

They were both silent for a long time.

Lexi was the first to speak. "You're right. There is no way out—it's just a matter of getting through the worst of it with the least pain."

Todd leaned backward in his chair and Lexi noticed how mature he looked for a boy his age. "It's a mistake not worth making."

When their eyes met across the table, Lexi's were

filling with tears. "I just wish I knew how to help Peggy through this."

Todd leaned across the table and rested his hand on Lexi's. "I know how you feel." Then he lifted a gentle finger to her cheek and wiped away a tear. "I do have some better news."

"Something that will cheer me up?"

"I think so. A little, anyway."

"Then what are you waiting for?"

"I saw Jerry at my brother's garage. He was working on his car."

"He's always working on his car. Why should that cheer me up?"

"He had a long talk with his parents."

"And?"

"And they've invited him to visit them this summer. And not just a short trip like he's had in the past. For three months."

"And Jerry?"

"He's excited, of course. He really laid it on the line about how he felt when they came for their 'visits' and then disappeared again. It must have had some impact."

"That's great, isn't it?"

"Jerry thinks so. I think the invitation diffused a real powder keg of trouble."

Lexi gave a weak smile. "Well, that's one problem on its way to being solved . . ."

"And another on its way," Todd finished for her. "I see Peggy coming up the back walk."

Lexi glanced out in time to see Peggy mount the steps. She disappeared from sight and a moment later the doorbell rang.

"I think I'd better be going," Todd whispered. "She doesn't want to talk to me." He grabbed his coat from the back of the chair. "Give me a second to get out the front." With that he disappeared into the hall. By the time Lexi got to the back door, she'd already heard the front door whisper shut. Peggy burst into the house in a breathless rush. "Are you alone?"

Lexi nodded. "Let's go into the living room."

Without answering Peggy fled through the hallway and flung herself onto the couch. For the first time, Lexi could see tearstains on her friend's cheeks.

"We were up all night," Peggy began, "my parents and I. It was like if we stayed up long enough and talked hard enough, we'd solve things!" She scrubbed at her eyes with the back of her hand. "Chad's parents have been really hard on him. I think they're afraid that the word will get out that I'm pregnant and it will embarrass the family."

"But what about you? Don't they care because of you?"

Peggy shook her head. "I doubt it. Chad's parents care more about protecting the family name than anything else. At least they won't be telling a lot of people what's happened!"

Lexi frowned. Already she didn't like Chad's family—and she hadn't even met them. Poor Peggy! After hearing that, Lexi was surprised that Chad had even offered to marry her.

Peggy was trembling.

"Do you need something, Peg? A drink of water? A—"

"All I need is to go back in time and undo what's

been done. To not be pregnant anymore. To erase the fact that I talked to Rita and she told Minda. To destroy every copy of the 'Review.' To—"

"And since that can't happen . . . what will?"

Peggy gave a gusty sigh. "My parents made telephone calls. I have an uncle in Arizona. A doctor. They want me to go and stay with him." Peggy grimaced as she added, "Before my pregnancy starts to show." She looked down at her flat belly in wonder, as if trying to imagine it as it would be in a few months.

"Is that what *you* want to do?"

Peggy shrugged. "I messed up by doing what I wanted to do. Now they think they'd better call the shots. They think that I should have time away from Chad. They're feeling guilty for letting things get this far out of hand, so now they say we shouldn't see each other." She looked at Lexi with pained eyes. "Crazy, isn't it? Now that it's too late, they want to make things right."

"Kind of, but I guess they think they have to do something."

Lexi curled her legs beneath her as she sat on the couch beside Peggy.

"They want to get me into counseling," Peggy said carefully. "My uncle told them he knows a counselor down there that he thinks can help me." Her unfocused gaze seemed to rest on the point where the wall met the floor. "If I give the baby up for adoption, they'll help me with that too. My mom thinks that with this arrangement I could even come back to school next fall without everyone knowing about the baby." She blinked. "Of course, no one counted on Minda's column."

"You don't have to worry about that," Lexi consoled. "I was in the staff room this afternoon. Mrs. Drummond is back and she knows what Minda did in the column. There's going to be a total retraction—for everything said, especially about the 'unfounded rumors' that Minda started. Minda can't write the next gossip columns and if there's any more trouble, she's off the staff entirely. Frankly, I think the whole thing will die down. The big news now is that Minda's in trouble. Everyone is speculating that she just made things up for shock value."

"Yeah, shock value. I'm good for plenty of that," Peggy groaned.

"So, are you going to go to Arizona?" Lexi asked. "For sure?"

Peggy nodded slowly. "I was going to be gone anyway. Dad is supposed to be in London soon and I was going with him and Mom but now . . ." Tears began to flood down Peggy's cheeks.

Lexi moved closer and put her arms around her friend. She could feel Peggy's shuddering sobs.

"Peg?"

Peggy rubbed her eyes again. "Now I'm going to my uncle's while they go to London. They've decided to tell people that I'm going to go to school in Arizona while they're gone. The baby will be due shortly after they get back." Peggy turned to Lexi with a pleading expression. "I really wanted to go with them, Lexi. I wanted so many things—London, being one of the starting five on the varsity team . . ." Her voice trailed away in a pitiful sob. "Now I've ruined everything! If it wasn't for God's forgiveness and love, I wouldn't even want to face the future."

Chapter Twelve

"Write? You'll promise to write? Absolutely? Before you do *anything* else?" Peggy's teary eyes were riveted to Lexi's face.

"Of course I will! You've given me three boxes of stationery and a roll of stamps!" Lexi tried to tease Peggy out of her weepy mood.

She and Peggy were huddled together at the foot of Peggy's bed. On the far side of the closed door were Peggy's suitcases. In less than an hour, her father would be home to drive her to the airport and Peggy would be gone.

"I can't believe I'm going, you know that? It doesn't seem real. When I said goodbye to Chad last night, do you know what he did?"

Lexi shook her head.

"He cried, Lexi. He actually cried. He apologized for what's happened to me—to us—and he said that when I get back next fall, he wants to start over and make things right."

"Do you?"

Peggy gave her head a bewildered shake. "I don't

121

know. All I know is that I can't get so deeply involved again. I won't get trapped in another problem like this one." She gave her stomach a rueful rub. "We know where that got me."

Lexi tried to smile. She wanted to say something but words escaped her.

"Todd's been great for Chad, you know. Just like you've been for me. You both have such a"—she searched for the right word—" . . . sturdy . . . kind of faith. You've made us both see that even though we've blown it, we can be forgiven and have another chance."

Lexi remained silent. Most of what she'd done the past few days was listen as thoughts and feelings poured out of Peggy like water from a tributary.

"I like what you said about 'all have sinned and fallen short of the glory of God,'" Peggy said. "I don't feel good about being a sinner, but at least I don't feel so alone."

"You aren't alone in that, I can promise you." Lexi laid a hand on Peggy's arm. "Everybody does wrong things. If we weren't sinners, then Christ wouldn't have had to die for us on the cross."

"Do you think the kids at school suspect?" Peggy wondered, her mind already flitting to another topic, much as it had for the past few days.

Patiently, Lexi shook her head. "Everyone knows your father is going to Europe and that you're going to stay with an uncle in Arizona while your parents are gone. I don't think anyone connects it with the possibility that you're pregnant. And you can be sure Todd and I won't tell."

"No. And I'm sure Chad won't. I think this has

shaken him up pretty badly."

"And you, Peg, how about you?"

"I'm shaken up too. I never thought I'd get myself into a mess so big I couldn't get out of it by myself, but I did." Peggy clutched Lexi's hand. "If it hadn't been for you and my parents . . . and God . . . I know I wouldn't have gotten this far. But I really feel like God is with me now, Lexi. He's going to Arizona with me even though you and my folks can't." Renewed tears came to her eyes. "That means that three of us are taking this trip."

"You, and God, and . . ."

" . . . the baby."

"What are you going to do, Peggy?"

"You mean about keeping it or giving it up?" Peggy sighed and sank onto the bed. "One day I think I'm keeping it for sure, no matter what anyone says or what happens, and the next I'm thinking that there's no way I could take care of a baby. I can't even imagine how it would be to have responsibility for another person twenty-four hours a day, seven days a week. Especially since I can't even seem to manage myself."

Lexi dropped silently onto the bed next to Peggy.

"I really do want to go to college," Peggy continued. "I suppose if I keep my baby I'll have to get a job and maybe I won't get to school." She wove her hands into a nervous tangle. "If I keep it, I've got to realize that I've got to take care of it. A baby isn't like a puppy you can advertise to give away in the newspaper. I guess I was pretty arrogant to think I could do whatever I wanted and assume I wouldn't hurt anyone else. Now I've hurt lots of people. Even someone who hasn't been born yet."

"Chad is a part of this too, you know," Lexi pointed out mildly. "He should be taking some responsibility for this."

"He's trying. But he can't offer a baby any more than I can right now. If we'd only waited . . ."

Peggy's head drooped and she gave a tired sigh. "I guess the counselors my uncle has lined up will help me decide. My uncle says he's had several patients in my situation. He told my parents that I should try to make up my mind before the baby's birth. He said it would be better if I were clearheaded and not all emotional." Peggy looked up and a tiny spark of hope lit her expression. "I'm going to ask God to help me decide, Lexi. Then I'll know that at least this time, I've made the right decision."

Suddenly, Peggy grabbed Lexi's hands and took them into her own. "Oh, Lexi, don't ever get into the mess I've gotten into!"

Lexi could feel her trembling. She wanted to tell Peggy that everything would be all right, but Lexi wasn't sure it would—at least not for a long, long time.

"I'll pray for you, Peg. And I'll write. Every week. I promise."

Peggy wiped away the tears that had coursed down her cheeks. She looked young and pitiful and in no way ready to be a mother.

"Peggy? Your father is home." It was Mrs. Madison, calling from the bottom of the stairs.

"I've got to go," Lexi murmured.

Peggy nodded. "This is it, then."

"Only for awhile."

"Keep Minda in line while I'm gone, will you?"

"That's a full-time job."

"I know, but somebody's got to do it."

They were both smiling through their tears by the time they reached the bottom of the stairs. Impulsively, Lexi leaned over and grabbed Peggy in a hard, quick hug. Without another word, she left the house.

Lexi was halfway down the block before she turned around to watch Peggy crawl into the backseat of her father's car. Lexi was almost home before she realized that there were tears running down her own cheeks and little sobs making her breathing ragged and uneven.

She looked at her watch. In less than an hour Peggy would be on her way to Arizona, leaving behind everything she'd cared so much about—Chad, the basketball team, her friends.

Then, with a sudden clearness that startled her, Lexi remembered one of the scripture verses that had been read in church the past Sunday.

> For I am sure that neither death, nor life, nor angels, nor principalities, nor things present, nor things to come, nor powers, nor height, nor depth, nor anything else in all creation, will be able to separate us from the love of God in Christ Jesus our Lord.

Peggy would be gone for awhile, that was true. But she wasn't going to be separated from the truly important One in life. No trouble would ever draw God away from her. He'd promised that. And Lexi was certain the same promise was true for her. Whatever happened, whatever turns their lives took, God would be with them.

Feeling more lighthearted than she had in days, Lexi looked up to see Binky coming down the sidewalk. Egg was beside her, talking and gesturing, waving his scrawny arms in the air. The more Egg gestured, the more deeply Binky frowned. It appeared they were on the verge of a big disagreement.

Lexi covered her face to hide the smile sneaking to her lips. Not everything had changed in Cedar River.

———

First Lexi loses her friend Peggy. Now Lexi's mother has gotten the crazy notion that she should put her mothering talents and energy into becoming a foster parent. Grown up as she feels she is, Lexi isn't ready to share her parents with strangers! How does Lexi handle this? Find out in Cedar River Daydreams #6.

A Note From Judy

I'm glad you're reading *Cedar River Daydreams*! I hope I've given you something to think about as well as a story to entertain you. If you feel you have any of the problems that Lexi and her friends experience, I encourage you to talk with your parents, a pastor, or a trusted adult friend. There are many people who care about you!

Also, I enjoy hearing from my readers, so if you'd like to write, my address is:

> Judy Baer
> Bethany House Publishers
> 6820 Auto Club Road
> Minneapolis, MN 55438

Please include an addressed, stamped envelope if you would like an answer. Thanks.